RESURRECTION TRUST

Edited by
Amanda Saint

Retreat West Books
https://retreatwestbooks.com

CONTENTS

FOREWORD

WE LIVE IN a beautiful world, with amazing wildlife, magnificent landscapes and inspiring oceans. I feel incredibly lucky to live in Brighton, within easy reach of the sea and the magnificent South Downs – both filled with life.

But in recent years my walks on the beach and over the hills have felt different. It's become clear that climate breakdown, industrial agriculture, pesticides and harmful practices are eradicating wildlife and sterilising habitats with frightening efficiency.

The swift – a bird that flies over one million miles – has seen its population cut in half in the last 20 years. In 1950, there were an estimated 36 million hedgehogs in the UK – now, that's dropped to around 1 million. Overall, more than one in ten of the UK's wildlife species is facing extinction, making us one of the most nature depleted countries in the world.

This annihilation is not just a tragedy for iconic species and future generations – it's a threat to our very survival. We depend on the natural world for everything – destroying it should be unthinkable.

With the world's top scientists telling us we have the tools and just enough time to turn things around, political will is all that stands in our way. To persuade governments around the world to act, we need to mobilise a mass movement.

Research by Dr Denise Baden from the University of Southampton, helps us understand what motivates people – and why so many of us have switched off. Catastrophic stories of the terrible consequences of climate breakdown can literally scare us stiff. We respond to our feelings of helplessness and fear by simply disengaging. But this anthology of short stories offers a different approach. Each writer presents a positive vision of transformative solutions that can help us live better lives and enhance our natural world.

The stories were sourced by a competition launched by Dr Baden (www.greenstories.org.uk) and the best ones have been selected for this anthology. Some explore the relationships between people and their environment. Others imagine futures where buildings are covered with plants and technology helps us to live sustainably. Some are exciting, some funny, some scary, some touching and some romantic – but they all suggest ways to live that are both more fulfilling and more sustainable.

These are the kinds of hopeful and inspiring visions we should be using to engage the public. It's going to take a transformation of our economy to secure our futures.

But with bold, positive campaigns and tangible ideas for change like these, I believe we can unite communities and persuade those in power to act.

Caroline Lucas
MP, Brighton Pavilion and former leader of the Green Party

ONE GREEN BOTTLE
Bridget Scrannage

PAUL BIT INTO his cheese and pickle sandwich and stared at the blank white board. What was it Mandy had said at the end of the nature documentary last week? 'Yeah, but they're just a bunch of freaky fish. Who cares about the eco-thingy anyway?' He sighed, swallowed and took another bite, barely registering that he was eating at all. How could he get through to these kids? Useless trying to scare into action a generation raised on apocalyptic computer games. Could they even discern genuine threats to survival from the fake ones constantly bombarding them on social media? They were immune, in emotional shutdown so engaging with them was close to impossible. How could he inspire a youngster in a world where the greatest measure of success was to win a reality TV show?

The classroom door banged open. A bundle of testosterone and arrogance by the name of Aidan swaggered in, followed by more fourteen-year-olds. Some were chatting, others staring zombie-like at their mobile phones.

Paul finished his sandwich and stowed its reusable beeswax wrapping back in his bag for the next day. Mandy arrived wearing a thick layer of make-up. She swigged the remainder of a fizzy drink from a green plastic bottle and chucked the empty container into the waste paper bin. Should he tell her to put it in the plastics recycling instead? He didn't have the energy, he'd do it himself later.

'OK,' he cleared his throat and stood up. 'Put those phones away.' As usual, some obeyed while others just carried on texting. 'Now.' The room settled and thirty disinterested faces turned towards him.

'Seen any good films lately?' Paul said.

A slight buzz went around the room. Some of the class sat a little straighter in their chairs.

'Yeah, Mandy's been watching that kissy-kissy sloppy stuff and fantasising about me, haven't you babes?' Aidan said. His cronies laughed.

'No way. Don't flatter yourself.' Mandy protested, a natural blush glowing beneath the artificial one.

'Okay,' 'how about films with aliens? Anyone like those?'

"A general chorus of approval rippled around the room.

'Are we going to watch one today?' Aidan said.

'It'd be better than them freaky fish,' Mandy said.

'Those freaky fish.' Paul corrected her grammar on

autopilot, then realising what he'd said, amended it to, 'Those fish. No, I just want to talk about the films.'

'Oh,' the buzz subsided.

'Does anyone enjoy films where aliens invade the Earth and destroy civilisation?'

'They're cool,' Aidan said.

'Yeah,' Mandy agreed.

'What do you like about them?' Paul said.

'Splattering the aliens,' Aidan said, making a fist with his right hand and using it to strike the open palm of his left.

'Saving the Earth,' Mandy said.

Bingo. 'Who saves the Earth?'

The class reeled off a predictable array of Hollywood A-Listers.

'How do they do it?'

'Guns.' Aidan said.

'Yeah, guns. Sometimes they've got to nuke 'em,' Mandy added.

'So when the Earth needs saving, a bloke with a gun is the one for the job. That right?'

'Yeah,' a general murmur of assent.

'How's the bloke with a gun going to save the Earth from climate change?'

Silence.

'Which is destroying it faster than any alien.'

More silence.

'Nuclear weapons aren't going to be much help here are they?'

Several heads shook.

'The Earth's being destroyed. The usual solution isn't working. Pretend you're writing the film. Who's your hero or heroine going to be?'

They looked at one another, nonplussed.

'Right, no hero. In the film the Earth will get destroyed then. Shall we send in the alien spaceships to rescue the human race?'

'That'd be cool,' a voice drifted from the back of the room. Ryan, a lanky wastrel who owed him coursework. He made a note on his desk pad to collar him before the class left.

'You'd be okay with that?'

'But isn't that like alien abduction?' Mandy said.

'They might experiment with your brain, Mandy,' Aidan said. 'If they can find one.'

The room exploded with laughter.

'So, Earth's been destroyed. Alien rescue's not a favourable, or likely, option. The film doesn't have a very happy ending, does it? Has anyone got a better script in mind?'

'Someone would have to do something,' Mandy said.

'Who would that someone be?' Paul prompted.

'A politician, I guess,' she said.

'Have you got faith in them?' Paul said.

'Urgh, no. My dad says they're a bunch of…'

'Whoa there, Mandy. I think we can guess how that sentence ends.'

'Idiots. I was going to say idiots,' she protested, then laughed.

'So, if not the politicians, then who?'

'Well, us, I s'pose,' Mandy conceded.

Jackpot. 'Correct answer. Us. Every single one of us gets to be the hero, heroine or villain in this film.' Paul said.

'I'll be the villain,' Aidan said.

'But they get nuked,' Mandy replied.

Nods of assent.

'So, going back to the freaky fish, what are we going to do to save them?'

Paul watched in astonishment as Mandy walked over to the waste paper recycling and retrieved the green bottle.

'Well, this can go in with the plastics for a start, Mr Dirham,' she said.

'One small step for the freaky fish; a giant leap for Mandy,' Ryan heckled.

The class cheered.

It was just one green bottle – but maybe one day there'd be ten, or more. Feeling a little foolish, Paul turned to write something on the white board so that the class wouldn't notice the tiny tear of joy he allowed himself to cry.

COME HELP ME

Nancy Lord

ON MAY 1, aboard the *Morning Star,* Yulia is learning the various meanings of May Day. In Russia she knew it as a major holiday. In the Soviet days it had meant speeches and parades in Red Square and, later, in her time, it was a nicer day for celebrating spring and workers. In America, Peter is teaching her, it involves putting flowers in a basket and dancing around a pole with ribbons and maybe, too, depending on who you are, Communist sympathizer or not, saying kind things about workers. But, more importantly for them now, *mayday* is all one word and is what she must shout into the radio if the boat is on fire or sinking. She should shout it three times in a row, and give the location.

This is how you work the radio, Peter has shown her. This is the emergency locater beacon, and this is how you turn it on, although it should turn on automatically if it goes underwater. This is the emergency life raft, and this is where you release it. These are our survival suits. Now we put soap on the zippers. Now we practice getting into them. Gumby is a rubber man, yes, from a cartoon. No, hood now. Zip all the way. Now we do it again, faster. He uses the timer on his big, complicated, good-under-water watch. Now you are dead of hypothermia, he says, if she is too slow to zip or can't get her hair tucked into the hood.

She is very confused, but, no, *mayday* has nothing to do with spring or flowers or workers. It is French. Peter says: *venez m'aider,* come help me.

Yulia can barely imagine her other life, the one that is disappearing with every minute on the water and every mile from land. Only two days ago – just when finals week started – she'd sold her textbooks, tossed piles of papers into the trash, kissed her favourite microscope goodbye, and flown to Kodiak to meet Peter. Her master's degree in marine biology and the award she'd received for her thesis were happy achievements, but she hadn't needed the long robe and flat hat nor so much hugging.

She has a new job: sticking hooks into stinky herring, clipping the short lines onto the long line. Watching the lines go down and then six hours later watching them come up, big white-belly fish taking shape as they swing towards the surface. Maggie's clothesline, Peter says. Like big white panties coming up, and it's for her to unpin them. Bigger than big panties – maybe pillow cases and sheets. Who is Maggie? Peter doesn't know this, just an expression.

Her happiness comes not just from big halibut that will make money for Peter and her. There is the rest to love: sky, waves, gulls with lonesome voices, some fish frying in a pan, a deck to scrub, a movie to watch and forget, mountains far away with snow. And Peter, of course: she wants to be with this man, her Petya, engine oil on his hands and fish oil in the brain.

Yulia is learning about the American enterprise system, quota shares that mean Peter can catch certain pounds of halibut in the part of the ocean called Area 3A. *Enterprising* is when you figure things out, like in science, but for more practical and personal reasons. Peter is always figuring things out, how to make something work, how to use mayonnaise instead of the eggs she somehow forgot at the store. She wants to be enterprising too, and now she has already learned how to run the hydraulics so that Peter can gaff the monster fish. When he was not mad about the eggs, he called her a natural at baiting hooks and snapping gangions. She felt proud when he praised her good hands. She is not so confident about knives. It's Peter's job to gut the fish, hers to pack the insides with ice. They will fill the hold this way.

Yes, all the weight of the school year, all the effort she'd made for so long – it falls away until she is like one of the gulls herself. That one, sitting on the water, riding up and over a swell, so lightly, like it is only feathers full of air.

'Dinner,' Peter calls through the open doorway. He's fixed sablefish – black cod, the fishermen call it, although it's not related to cod at all. Butterfish, Peter says the marketing people call it, selling its richness. She doesn't know the Latin, the genus, and maybe she doesn't care. 'Like candy,' Peter says now, delivering a steamy chunk to his open mouth. He's cooked it his favourite way – marinated in soy and ginger and broiled in the oven.

'Better than candy.' Yulia pushes aside a pile of clothing to sit opposite Peter at the galley table.

'Better than sex?'

'I don't think so.'

'It's an expression,' Peter says. 'You like something a lot, you say it's better than sex.'

Peter enjoys teaching her American idioms. Already that day: An old man kicked the bucket, he is bending over backwards, don't leave me high and dry. She likes visualizing all these – a person bent like a circle hook, someone on a mudflat with the tide gone out. How is being dead like kicking a bucket?

'You are a wet blanket,' she says. 'You are spilling beans. *Zamorish chervachka.*'

Peter cocks his head.

'You are not giving enough to eat to the little worm.'

'What little worm?'

Yulia shrugs. 'In your stomach? It means you eat only a little. Maybe not you. Someone else.'

'Definitely not me. I am eating high off the hog. I am the big enchilada.'

'I am the fish taco,' she says.

'Yes,' Peter says. 'You are definitely the fish taco.'

They're both quiet for a while, rocking in the swell while, down under, their baited hooks are swaying off the bottom, calling in the big halibut. Peter has been thinking about worms, because now he starts to talk about whale falls and what eats them, the ecosystems they support on the ocean floor, new species always being discovered. '*Osedax*,' Peter says. 'Bone-eating worms. There's one called the bone-eating snot flower. Not a flower, of course, but a worm that burrows into whale bones and has these pink flowery plumes.'

Yulia smiles. What was the chance that this man with rice in his beard would have found a woman as interested as he is in whale falls and worms and likes to talk about them during dinner? Her heart swells a little at the idea of their so-not-Russian and so-not-American match – and then at the beauty of whale falls. That dead whales sink into the dark abyss and then feed such amazing collections of creatures that will, over decades, recycle every bit of flesh and bone back into the living world – well, that is Nature at its most stunning efficiency. She says to Peter, 'Such great whale lipids.'

Everybody loves whales, but Yulia understands why most of them do not care to learn about worms. Worms do not have economic value or feed species that do. Decomposing whales do not help the whale-watching industry. That is something she learned in her years at university; you had to study something for which there was funding, and funding only came to projects that had economic value. Her professor had told her that over and over again: *You have to say, right here in your abstract and then again in your conclusion and summary, why* Metridia pacifica *is important in the food web. You have to discuss the significance of its rate of growth, its health or decline.* All those words: about copepods making up to eighty percent of metazoan biomass in the marine environment, the link from primary production to upper trophic levels. Trophodynamics. Bioindicators. *Say more, say it explicitly.* Fish and whales and birds eat them. *Yes, fish are the economy. People care about fish.* Her professor pulled out his hair about this. This was not an expression; he literally put his hands in his hair and pulled at it.

Now she cares about fish. Someone is going to give them money for halibut. The fish are in the ocean and belong to Nature, but soon they will be on their boat and belong to Peter and her. That is American enterprise. It is regulated, for sure. They can only take so much, the quota Peter owns, so that the fish make more fish. That is called "sustainable fishing practices".

Peter has gone off to his collection of dog-eared *National Geographics* to find an article he remembers about the Monterey Canyon, with photos of *Osedax* species on whale bones. His muffled voice, coming from the fo'c'sle, is saying, 'sexual dimorphism'.

Yulia takes their plastic plates to the tiny sink and washes them. Her professor, who loves all the creatures in the sea, pulls his hair out when he sees what is happening to the ocean—the "blob" of warm water in the North Pacific, the southern species moving north, the other species diving deeper to find cooler water, the acidification dissolving the shells of his cherished pteropods. She was supposed to go on his spring research cruise, and now she is one more disappointment to him.

It had simply come to her one day that she was no longer looking forward to more oceanography, in fact did not want to net the same samples again, did not want to count eggs again, did not want to squint into more bouncing microscopes or teach undergraduates the difference between *Neocalanus cristatus* and *Neocalanus flemingeri*. Yes, it is interesting what these species are doing, and yes, the time series are very important to understanding what's happening in the ocean, but she is not excited anymore about doing the same work over and over, while everything on the planet is in a toilet bowl, swirling down.

When Peter returns with the magazines, she says, 'I

am feeling a little guilted.'

'About the cruise?'

'It is starting in one week.'

'It was your idea to come fishing,' Peter reminds her. 'This is also a good skill, to know how to catch fish, and to run a boat. You'll have many arrows in your quiver.'

Yulia will be happy to have arrows in her quiver, whatever that is, but what she doesn't have is a life plan. For a long time she had thought she would take her American education back to Russia. But lately the news from home is not so happy; the Arctic institute she thought she'd work at doesn't have money even for sample jars, and its boats are always broken down, their motors so old there aren't even replacement parts. Russian politics are very strange, stranger even than in America. Her parents said, better to stay in America if she can. If she leaves, she might never be allowed back. She has, right there on the boat with her, applications for several doctoral programs.

'You will never be hungry, if you know how to fish,' Peter says.

'Until there aren't any fish,' she says.

Peter plants a wet kiss on her forehead. 'You have the very attractive Russian soul. Always suffering.'

YULIA PUTS ON warmer clothes and comes back on deck.

'They found us,' Peter says, handing her the binoculars. 'Sperm whales.'

Yulia follows their tilty blows as they advance towards the *Morning Star*. Three, four big whales, one perhaps smaller than the others.

'Oh, crap,' Peter says.

'Why oh crap?'

'Oh crap, that's the end of our black cod. You'll see. These guys belong in deeper water, chasing squid. But they've followed us in here over the shelf. Like flies to fish camp.' Peter is excited, not in a bad way.

The sky has darkened some, with a cloud pattern she knows is called mackerel, after a fish with big, shimmery scales. The light on the water shimmers in a similar way, blue and darker blue. Yulia watches the big whales slide alongside them, just boat lengths away. They settle there, long islands of backs catching the slippery light. Their breath becomes soft murmurings, like a roomful of dreaming babies.

Yulia has never seen, except in pictures, a sperm whale. In books, she has seen drawings of Moby-Dick bashing his big square head into boats, making them into wood splinters, people falling from the boats with screaming mouths. This is very different. This is a world at rest. She remembers fin whales she saw on her last research cruise, passing under their boat, the same feeling she had, something like what she imagines other people find in their religions. To know there is more than you can understand. And that not everything is about killing, although everything has to eat.

Peter is going on, quietly for Peter, talking about whale intelligence. Yulia is not hearing all of it. She is a scientist; she has learned not to say that any animals are intelligent. Whales have large and specialized brains – that is what science says. They make vocalizations and form social units. They often cooperate when feeding.

Peter and Yulia take a nap, same as the whales. Then, after coffee, it's time to haul gear. Deck lights. Hydraulics. The whales are not close now. Their blows are maybe a quarter-mile in front. Peter gaffs the first halibuts aboard, two in the thirty-pound range. A black cod, a halibut, then a dozen empty hooks and a dogfish with eyes like green marbles. Peter shakes that one off. A bigger halibut and a grey cod, a real cod. No more black cod. The whales are still in front, keeping the same distance.

'You see what's happening?' Peter yells to her. 'They're one step ahead of us as we pick up the skate. As soon as the line's coming up taut, they're snatching the fish.'

'Black cod is their favourite.'

'Yes, they're selective. Some guys say they lose halibut to them, too. I don't know. I think this first skate is pretty good for us. I think it's easy to blame bad fishing on a whale.'

Peter is shoving another halibut across the deck. Snot is dripping from his nose. 'How can you blame whales? We invent technologies to catch fish, the whales invent ways to use the same technology. It's adaptation. You'd do the same thing if you saw a bunch of tasty dishes going by you, like in those sushi restaurants where the little dishes are going around.'

Peter talks and talks about whales – killer whales that kill larger whales, humpback whales that sing, beluga whales with necks they can turn to look at you. Now he's a philosopher. 'We almost killed the big whales off because we didn't understand what we were doing and what value they might have besides grease and oil. But now they're back. You see, it's possible to turn things around.'

What Yulia can see is a very big difference between what was simple in the past and what is no longer simple now. Stop sticking harpoons and bombs into whales and fewer whales die. Now, nothing has one cause or easy fix. Sometimes her boyfriend can be a simpleton – or in America, what they call an optimist. This is maybe why she loves him. He believes that nothing is impossible.

PETER LIKES TO talk on the marine radio to the other boats. On one channel he talks to his friends, and they share information about where they're fishing. Maybe they lie about what they're catching – or maybe they don't. On other channels, with other fishermen, it's just bullshitting. Now he's telling someone they're running east, trying to leave the whales behind. Let the whales find some other boat to dine with. Now he's telling someone else about ocean acidification. 'No, man, this is real. This is happening now. It's chemistry.'

Some other fishermen want to argue with him. They tell him they heard that fishing would be shut down to protect some stupid little snail. They know that the real source of acidification is from underwater volcanoes. They insist that acidification is not a problem because climate change is fake science and, besides, everything can adapt.

'Where do you get this shit?' Peter yells at them. 'No one's talking about shutting down fisheries. It would be smart to let the science people study the effects, though, and think about managing for resilience. Yes, *resilience*. Like *resilient*. No, I'm not going all dome-headed highbrow! It's a word! Get used to it.'

Peter has always said that one reason he likes being on the boat is that he can always think clearly there. His best ideas come in the motion between sky and sea, in the big hum that is more than engine noise. He turns to Yulia now. 'We need to write some of this stuff down. Fact sheets. You know, the chemistry with the molecules and the cycling arrows and the pH scale and rate of change. And stuff about fish. What everything eats.'

'Yes,' she says. 'Let's do that!' She is thinking of her sad professor and the others – the ocean chemists with their papers and slides. They talk to themselves, the bad news about the ocean, the way everything connects, what needs to happen to protect their ocean home. Someone needs to talk to *other* people. Her Petya is a good talker.

Ideas are pouring out of him now. As soon as they have a load, they'll deliver to Kodiak, print and copy fact sheets and science papers, walk the docks. Peter knows the fishermen, and Yulia knows the science. They'll give presentations in the schools, at the Rotary meeting, in the churches. They'll go on local radio. Pretty soon there won't be a soul in Kodiak who doesn't know what a pteropod is and why it's important.

'And why it is threatened,' Yulia adds.

'And why it's threatened.'

They'll need to come back out for more halibut and then get ready for salmon season, but Peter has an idea about that, too. He's going to start an organization called Ocean Witnesses. Fishermen and anyone else who works on the water will start collecting their own data, doing their own documentation. This will be about climate change and ocean acidification, both. When they catch an oddball fish – something out of its range or with a freakish deformity – they'll report this. They'll take photos and videos and post them. They'll collect water samples. The scientists can tell them what to observe and collect; they'll work together. The scientists can't always be on the water. The fishermen will be eyes and ears, witnesses and reporters, truth tellers.

It is a grand plan!

They sleep on it, and the next day Peter has another idea. At the beginning of salmon season, before they scatter, the Kodiak fleet will do 'an action'. The tenders and the seine boats and the setnet skiffs, pleasure boats and kayaks too, will gather outside the harbour and line up to make big OA letters with a circle and a slash, or maybe more words than that – NO ACID OCEAN, perhaps – depending on how many boats participate. Peter knows a guy with a drone, who'll take photos to put on the internet and everywhere. They'll invite the governor. They'll invite that crazy loon of a congressman. Those people love public events. They'll make a hell of a splash.

'We'll get artists to make art,' Yulia adds. 'Banners to hang from the seagull nests.' She's not sure she's used the right name for the top part of the boat, but it's something like that and Peter doesn't correct her.

'Yes, lots of art, and lots of music.' Peter's voice has gotten louder and louder. 'A big seafood feast at the end! That's what it's all about! The ocean that feeds us!'

Who will do all these things? Yulia doesn't know, but Peter is already on the radio, organizing. 'Yes, Ocean Witnesses,' he's saying. 'I'm signing you up.'

Yulia watches him in his captain's chair: wild hair sticking up, sleeves rolled to elbows, eyes set on the horizon. He's seeing the future, or *a* future, one with fish and whales and, of course, copepods – her copepods. She tries to think of an American way to say this. He is over the rainbow. Maybe he is over the moon. He is a fish in water. Or maybe a bridge over troubled water. That is a song she's heard. She reaches out to squeeze his arm. The world is calling to Peter, and he is going to help.

THE RETURN
Meg Smith

AT 5 A.M. the world seemed brighter, despite the surrounding blackness. Grass, wet with dew, tickled my bare feet. Scanning for snakes I walked along the bank, long spear held ready, my legs tense with anticipation.

A quick glimmer, like a trick of the eye.

With a practiced manoeuvre I launched the spear forward, my fingers tracing its trajectory. Water splashed up from the stream, cold on my legs. With a fond thought of long-past hiking books, I slid one foot into the icy water. "Brrr."—the sound arose from me like a complaint against the earth itself. Now the next one. Knowing what was coming made it worse.

Wading slowly, I reached my spear and looked hopefully into the gently moving mirror of water.

'Damnit.' I scowled at the water, my anger reflecting uselessly back at me.

I yanked the spear out of the water, momentarily considering cracking it over my knee, and moved back towards the bank. It's not breakfast time yet.

My stomach grumbled, anyway. With a sigh I turned towards home, keeping an eye out for small red berries, a prey even I could catch.

Mounting the last hill before camp, I heard the argument before I saw it:

'Call the government and FORCE them to put it all back!'

'It isn't as simple as that…what could we even CALL them with?'

'We all know you're hiding an iPhone in the head tent. Don't even try to deny it!'

'All modern technology was confiscated for the Return, you know that.'

'All I know is that when they told us we would be returning to a better time, no one in their right mind was thinking of THIS.'

Round and round went the argument: we didn't know what we were doing, and now we want to go back. Except there was no 'back' to go back to. Nothing remained. The Return had been complete. Each country's metaphorical time clock set backward, the land terraformed to a pre-determined era, the re-do we thought we wanted.

Sometimes I wondered how the other eras were doing; I think I felt the most sympathy for those returned to the Pleistocene, the last ice age. My own return, to the end of the Pliocene, had felt like happy circumstance. The loss of large reptiles, warm temperatures, and forest life. How poetic, right? This is the moment before a human-like species separated from the monkeys—this is THE moment. Well, it turns out THE moment is less like paradise than we thought.

'Can't you see? This ISN'T working. It's failed. We're done.'

The head of our group, a woman chosen before the Return, remained calm. 'We've been here for two years. Most of us have survived the adjustment and are beginning to adapt to the new environment. We haven't failed.'

The lack of fresh fish in my stomach was like a sharp ache when she spoke of adapting to the new environment. I knew we weren't supposed to progress, that the goal was to create a contented stasis, but my stomach wanted to fashion a 21st century net and scoop up five fish at a time.

Spotting Daiya, I squeezed in next to her to watch the end of the argument.

'Hey, Zeya,' she whispered, looking at me sideways, keeping an eye on the middle of the circle.

'Hey. Who is it this time?'

'Leila and the gang. Again.'

I nodded conspiratorially. Leila always wanted to go back, and she had no trouble convincing others to back her up.

'Fine. We can't go back. But that doesn't mean we

can't go forward. We all know what the future's supposed to look like, let's speed up this timeline by about two million years.'

A groan spread throughout the onlookers.

'Repetition isn't the answer. We were only given one Return and we can't repeat our mistakes.'

'We were *fine*. Everyone had TVs and food and cars and *freedom* to do whatever we pleased. You might call it a mistake but I don't have to agree.'

I knew the speech before the headwoman started talking. Plastic pollution, the melting ice caps, abundant waste, mass extinctions. I tuned her out. Knowing all that then hadn't changed a thing, and knowing it now wouldn't change the minds of hungry people faced with foraging for food.

I wasn't exactly sure where I stood. I remembered the pollution, even though the time before felt distant and fuzzy now.

As the headwoman's speech drifted off, so too did the members of the crowd. Off to their lives, hunting, gathering, living.

***

THE ROARING BLARE of a siren screeching past wrenched me from sleep. Rolling over I looked at the clock: 5 a.m. 'Nooo....' I moaned. *One more hour, come on, Zeya, you can do this.* I lay and counted the tiny mounds on the popcorn ceiling, then fumbled clumsily for the remote. The overly perky voice of a news anchor filled the room. Rubbing my eyes, I stared at the screen.

'...reports say that there is more plastic than fish in the ocean...'

'...a new species of spider has just been found...'

'...new species of spider dies out just hours after discovery...'

'...new make-up brush made of 100% biodegradable plastic...'

Half-listening, I made my way to the kitchen. Coffee filter, coffee, water, on.

***

THE NIGHT SKY glittered in the deep black of the pre-industrial forest. Or was it pre-post-industrial? Talking about time had gotten complicated, tied in knots by linear language.

What did I think when they made the announcement? Was I pleased? The world was. It was the ultimate reset button.

'A special report from the United Nations. Scientists in Switzerland believe they have found the cure for global warming. Operation Return will reroute the Earth's climate patterns, pull up the skeletons of past lifeforms, and facilitate

the re-implementation of flora to reconstruct the different geological epochs on top of the current one. Humanity gets a second try.'

Moving forward to go back to square one. There were protestors. Those who felt that terra-forming the planet could have untold consequences. Who felt that impoverished nations didn't have a say. Who saw this not as a solution, but as an escape.

Most of us wanted an escape.

It had been difficult to ignore the odd tinge to the skies, the way fisherman caught milk jugs as often as halibut, the protestors outside Starbucks, demanding the end of single-use anything. Well, as it turns out, they got what they wanted. We fixed the problem of a single-use Earth.

Flames danced in the darkness. Were we allowed to have fire? Was this technology beyond our epoch? We were floundering after our historian died. Despite the anachronism, we were all glad to be warm, even the headwoman. Sitting up, I squeezed mud between my toes. I often wondered how old this dirt was. Was it dredged up in the Transition, pulled out of the heart of the Earth? Was it topsoil, the old foundation of a backyard in Pennsylvania? Or was it the GMO-dirt, mass-produced to cover up what we didn't want seen? I preferred to think it was the old stuff, filled with memory and age. It felt like shadow solidified under my feet.

TAKE LID OFF oatmeal, pour in water, microwave for two minutes. Was the container recyclable? I tossed it in the trashcan on my way out the door; I'd look at it later.

Walking down the street was different now. Full of people, empty of the groans, putters, and shrieks of cars inching by in traffic. I looked down at my shoes, blue flats with black rhinestones, surrounded by a banana peel with the label still on, a movie stub, lone playing card, plastic coffee lid.

Shit! I forgot coffee. And my travel mug. I looked around like someone might be witnessing my moral failing. Finding no judgemental eyes, I popped into the nearest coffee shop.

'One triple Americano, to go.'

'Do you have your own cup?' The barista asked, looking bored, with a marker poised over a plastic coffee cup.

'No.' Did I look guilty?

'Name?'

'Zeya.'

She scribbled furiously and moved on. I teetered side to side, waiting.

I darted back out the door. I couldn't throw it away at the office, much too risky. It was my week as Recycling Monitor. I chugged the Americano in a park near work, shoving the empty cup into a nearby bin, burying it with the other rubbish.

***

I KICKED AT a rock near the streambed, unplugging it from the watery clay, looking for fossils, wondering if fossils existed, or if we were the fossils. The rock teetered over.

'Nothing,' said Daiya, who had wandered over. 'Again.'

'Some of this dirt is old, some of it has to remember,' I said, squinting at her face in the sun.

'So what if it does?'

Sometimes I wondered if we were supposed to learn something. That this wasn't just some grand experiment in human evolution. "*Given the different flora, fauna, and climates of the 9 epochs, each group should adapt separately, revising evolutionary patterns…*"

What if you couldn't revise the human instinct to consume? Particularly at the expense of others. Separate from the system but parasitically mooching off of it. What if that was our biological drive? What if Darwin was right, but our best chance for survival was parasitism? In the forest, it was hard to miss. Even in competition the forest ecosystem supported itself: nutrients created, used, passed on, absorbed, changed, recreated.

I looked around at the members of my group, picking berries, gathering firewood, collecting stones for crafts.

What did we contribute?

***

I LOOKED DOWN at my smart watch: 7,345 steps, 5:12 p.m.

My car seemed wreathed in emissions; we were being encouraged to use public transport as much as possible before the Return. Something about maintaining stable atmospheric conditions for the scientists. But the bus didn't go to the pub, didn't even get near it. So I'd have to walk the mile to the pub, and the mile home. Just one mile in a car (okay, two), wouldn't even leave a blemish on those scientists' machines.

I felt conspicuous as I turned on the too-loud engine, its sound echoing in the alley. I backed into the nearly empty street.

Not even a blemish.

***

WE WEREN'T SURE if we were allowed to write. Since our historian had died we were making things up as we went.

'We can't ignore that we all know how to write. It might be a technology, but the tools we have to create the texts with are still minimal.' The headwoman looked out over the group. No one disagreed; we all wanted to write.

We sat around the fire in various positions of studi-ousness, using charcoal bits from last night's fire to write on leaves and rocks and pieces of bark. Is this what we contributed? Transformation? Under the human eye a piece of charcoal was a tool for creating text and the bark from a tree was the container, the receiver, of that text. We saw what was there and what it could be.

I wrote: 'Dejr Mom,'

'Damnit.'

I tried to erase the charcoal lettering with the back of my hand. It smudged over the entire piece of bark, creating a night scene. Groaning, I unbent myself and walked over to another tree, using a rock to break away a piece of the skin. It peeled back intimately, like I was revealing the naked tree underneath.

'Dear Mom,' I was more careful this time. 'I'm loving the forest here, it's so lush and green…'

It felt sort of pat, too mundane for charcoal and bark. She was only in the village on the other side of the valley, I could see her tomorrow. The piece of bark felt heavy in my hands. The open white patch on the tree across the camp glowed over the morning flames.

Why did it feel like nothing had changed?

***

THE RETURN WAS tomorrow. That was like saying the apocalypse was tomorrow. There were no rules, no society. Despite the requests of the Swiss scientists, asking us to not exacerbate the Earth's problems with radical consumption changes, it felt like the day before the Shemittah year, sweeping away not just 7 years, but 12,000 years of human debt.

***

I CAN'T REMEMBER the actual Return. It felt like waking up exactly where you expected to find yourself, no mental whiplash. Sure, there was a learning curve. But now things had settled into a comfortable familiarity. Looking around at the vibrant green of the dense underbrush, feeling the rough textured bark of a tree under my hand, the forest felt like home.

Some people had wanted to chop down the trees, to make larger houses like log cabins. But again, the headwoman had stepped in, reminding us about the rules for using technology beyond our epoch, even though it felt like that was sort of a lost cause.

The camp was humming with news. Tomorrow we'd visit one of the other groups from our epoch, to compare lifestyles and check in. It wasn't one we had ever visited before. What would their camp look like? Had they fudged on any technology use? Basically, how did our group stack up?

The sun was just turning the tips of the trees green when we set out. It was about ten miles to the neighboring camp. Progress was slow through the dense vegetation; we paused to watch for animals, moving carefully to avoid the thorny vines weaving through the forest floor.

The sky was bright and the sun high as we approached the grassy meadow where the other camp had settled. A small area, islanded on three sides by trees and on one side by the smooth water.

'Where's the camp?' someone whispered.

The headwoman held up a hand, indicating we should stop.

'Look.' She pointed to where the grass met the forest edge. I squinted, the sun seemed to make everything too sharp, so that it was almost hazy. A head popped out the earth.

Someone else said, 'What?'

With a cheerful wave, the headwoman started towards the head. The rest of us followed more slowly. Where was the rest of the group? Where did they live?

They came into the clearing with a grace and seamlessness, like the reverse of evaporation. Out of doors built in between tree trunks and mounds of dirt only a few feet high.

'They've gone native,' whispered Leila.

It struck me the way she whispered it. So arrogantly, from up on high, as if she would never stoop to the level of disintegrating into the land. I pondered her exceptionalism; where *was* the human place? And did going native mean losing something innately human? And was that so bad?

The other group's leader, an androgynous figure of about five foot seven, greeted us: 'Hello, and welcome to our camp.'

Our headwoman's eyes sparkled, 'Thank you.' Eager for information, she asked, 'How do you live? What is this?'

She led us around the camp, pointing out the geographies of their way of life. Their camp was integrated, that was the word their leader had used.

'Some of us live in wood houses, like this,' she gestured towards the edge of the forest, where what looked like dense growth was actually a mixture of living trees and dead ones. The dead trees had been positioned vertically to fill in the gaps between living trees, creating a sort of circular shape.

'The existing forest canopy acts as a roof.' Smiling, she added, 'It isn't perfect,' as a few drips fell off the branches from last night's rainfall.

'Some of our members prefer to live underground, in burrows.' A small mound of grass rose vaguely out of the meadow, a subtle indicator of the human dwelling.

'What about food?' our headwoman asked, her eyes searching about for an explanation.

'We have small gardens for each of the ecosystems in our camp. Our forest gardens provide berries and roots and our water gardens allow certain greens to flourish.'

'What about your dead? I don't see a cemetery.'

'The dead are buried without coffins, dotted throughout the forest. It's circular.'

Progress in stasis. Moving forward but backward.

***

PERHAPS THIS EVOLUTIONARY moment wasn't the moment I thought it was. Perhaps it was a different sort of moment. The moment when man diverted, mentally assumed a different trajectory. The trajectory was divisive, parasitic. It wasn't circular, but linear.

Five....

Four....

Isn't a countdown a bit juvenile? Like the scientists have read one too many science fiction novels.

Three...

Maybe I should turn the TV off. Enter the Return not staring blindly into a bright screen.

Two...

Click. The TV flickered black and the voice stopped.

One

***

THE GROUP WAS hushed as we walked back to our camp. There was the vague feeling in the air that we had been reprimanded, a stern reminder of why we were here.

The forest dampness filled my pores, and the faint

mouldy smell of leaves underfoot seemed to clear my head.

It's circular.

What do we *contribute*?

RESURRECTION TRUST

Brian Burt

RIGEL CREPT THROUGH the forest understory as if it were a minefield. The Rez reminded him of a teenage sex artist he knew back in the Steel City of Kort: beautiful, mysterious, but deadly to those who let their guard down. Rigel knew better. His head swivelled at every chirp and chitter, vigilant amber eyes darting to track each rustle of foliage, snap of twig, crackle of dried leaves. The Rez was a dangerous place. It had swallowed more poachers than anyone could count in its verdant maw. He didn't intend to become another ghost haunting a cemetery marked by trees instead of gravestones. His dead mother's voice echoed in his head: 'Careful, Gel. Remember what I taught you. Respect the Rez, tread lightly and live to tell the tale.'

The mongrel mix of hardwoods and conifers gradually gave way to an orderly stand of pines, a bark-girded parade of soldiers standing at attention, awaiting Rigel's inspection. Yes! This was what he'd come for, despite the risks. He inhaled, savouring the scent of pine needles mingled with the sweet, seductive aroma of...something else. He spotted a branch drooping under the weight of its bounty. He moved closer, gaze never wavering from the prize. Half a dozen swollen cones hung below the branch. They looked like regular pine cones injected with liquid, like balloons about to burst. He plucked one from its stem, picked the scales from its bloated side, exposing the succulent flesh of the fruit hidden underneath the protective armour. He took a bite. Golden syrup dribbled down his chin. Ambrosia! So much better than the hydroponic fruits and vegetables grown in the Steel City's vertical gardens, or the bland, vat-grown meats generated layer upon layer in the protein factories.

One of these bioengineered honeycones held enough nutrients to keep him alive for days. A dozen, sold on the black market, would pay his living expenses for a month.

He slipped the pack from his back and began pulling ripe honeycones from the nearest trees, arranging them meticulously in the pack's main storage compartment. When he'd filled the pouch to bulging, he sealed it and pressed the button to evacuate its air, preserving his precious cargo for the return trip to Kort. Smiling. He'd be rich soon.

Then iron fingers gripped his collar bone. The hand turned him, slowly, until he stared into the grim, weathered face of a Ranger.

'You're trespassing on the sovereign lands of the Resurrection Trust, *maiaginini*. I'm taking you into custody, along with the contraband you've harvested. Hand me the pack and come with me. Don't make it worse.'

Rigel appraised the tall, wiry man with sharp, sombre eyes and decided discretion was the better part of valour. He surrendered his backpack, fighting the urge to clutch it tighter, and fell into step beside the Ranger, hoping he'd get a chance to a make a break for freedom later. The trees crowded closer, pitiless spectators gathered to witness a public execution.

THEY'D BEEN HIKING for at least an hour when the Ranger led Rigel to the edge of a shallow stream. He knelt, motioning Rigel to do the same. 'Drink. We still have a way to go, and the heat is deceptive, even in the shade.'

Rigel crouched beside the older man, studying him as discreetly as he could: jet black hair peppered with grey, tied back in a ponytail; dark, haunted eyes; ageless, angular features; a ragged scar tracing the curve of his jawline. His skin and clothes blended subtle shades of tan and brown, painted with the camouflage palette of the forest.

The Ranger sensed Rigel's sideways glance and sighed. 'Stop staring and start hydrating, son. We need to get moving.' He dipped his own cupped hands into the water, lifted them to his mouth. 'See? It's safe. Plenty of things on the Rez to kill you, but this stream isn't one of them.'

Rigel drank deeply. The water was clear, sweet, deliciously cool. No taint of chemicals; no tang of recycling or sterilization. He savoured it, suppressing a pang of jealousy. *You Rezzies have no idea how lucky you are.*

The Ranger read his mind. 'Not as tidy as the Steel Cities, but life here has its advantages. What's your name?'

'Rigel. But everybody calls me Gel.'

'Fair enough, Gel. My name is Joseph, but everybody calls me Two-Gee.'

'Two-Gee?'

'Long story. Don't want to bore you with it... not yet, anyway. Let's go.'

'Where are you taking me?' Rigel couldn't keep the quaver out of his voice. He'd heard plenty of stories about the fate of captured poachers on the Rez. None of them had happy endings.

'Where you need to go,' said Joseph. 'Not much farther. Consider it part of your penance for trying to steal from us.' Joseph gave his prisoner a speculative look, not exactly warm but far from hostile. 'I'm not your enemy, no matter what you've heard. Plenty of things on the Rez to kill you, but I'm not one of them.'

ANOTHER THIRTY MINUTES and the terrain changed. The forest thinned a bit; the ground became hillier, more rugged. Rigel considered himself fit, but he struggled to keep pace. They crested a knoll and stopped. A hollow spread out below them, filled with ferns and brush. A trail zigzagged through the undergrowth, meandering towards the hill that rose on the opposite side. Across that tree-covered hillside, Rigel spotted dozens of strange, circular windows and transparent oval doors embedded in the earth.

'What the hell?' muttered Rigel.

'We call it Odéna. I think your friends in the Steel City call it the Burrow.'

Rigel sighed. 'You gonna lock me in a cave?'

'Not yet. Maybe after the tour.'

Rigel followed Joseph along the twisting path to the excavated edges of the village.

'We dig our shelters into the hillside because the earth provides natural insulation; warmth in the winter, cooling in the summer. The doors and windows aren't glass or plastic, they're made from layered tree resin from the sealant-cedars that grow all over the Rez. We coat the inside of our chambers and connecting tunnels with the sap to stabilize the walls. Once it crystalizes, the stuff is waterproof and stronger than lucite.'

A weird hum emanated from the trees sprinkling the hillside, vibrating the vertebrae along Rigel's spine.

'What's that buzzing? Some kinda bug?'

'No,' said the Ranger. 'That's our power supply.'

'I thought the Rez was off the grid?'

'Off *your* grid. We have our own. These trees are electric-elms, genetically tweaked to do double duty. Why try to re-invent solar energy collectors when Mother Nature does it better than we ever could? These trees don't just photosynthesize the old-fashioned way, they divert surplus energy to special tissues in their trunks that store bio-electricity. Their root systems interconnect and work like buried power lines. Groves of e-elms are our private grid. The juice collected in the battery tissues protects the trees, fries pests that try to burrow beneath the bark. The root network is vast, intricate, and fault tolerant. If a storm knocks down some trees, replacements grow in time; until then, the grove-grid routes the flow of current around the damaged zone.'

Rigel couldn't hide his amazement. 'Wicked. We have brownouts in our sector of Kort at least twice a week.'

'No brownouts – or green-outs – on the Rez. The forest is dynamic and resilient.' As the two of them walked along the hillside, a few villagers waved from the shadows where they groomed the facades of buried shelters, tinkered with equipment, cleared encroaching brush, or did other communal chores. A few. Not many.

'Where is everybody?' asked Rigel.

'We're a border outpost. Most are out patrolling.

Those who aren't officially in the ranks have other duties: planting, foraging, harvesting, hunting.'

Rigel's stomach growled. 'Hunting? What, deer or turkeys? Real, wild game?'

'You've worked up an appetite, eh? Figured you for a carnivore. Hungry for some fresh meat?'

'Anything not grown in a lab!'

Joseph pointed. 'One of my fellow Rangers lives over that rise. She should be back from her rounds, usually cooks lunch about this hour. Let's join her.'

They topped the rise. A rocky hillside descended beneath them, dappled by shards of sunshine filtering through the canopy. Birds sang strident warnings to each other overhead. Squirrels and chipmunks chittered, scolding the two-legged invaders. The eerie background hum of e-elms mingled with the whisper of the wind. The Ranger led Rigel down a barely discernible trail through ferns, brush, and brambles. Rigel stumbled. It took all his concentration to avoid the stinging nettles and grasping thorny vines. He barely noticed how far they'd hiked before the first whiff of cooking meat caressed his nostrils. They swung around the trunk of an ancient oak and came upon a clear patch of stony ground covered with a patina of moss. In the centre, a woman bent over a battery-powered camp stove jacked into an exposed e-elm root. She gripped the handle of a skillet, shaking it from side to side. Whatever she was cooking smelled delicious. Rigel wiped a trace of drool from the corner of his mouth.

'Hi, Dub-Dub,' said Joseph. 'Have enough for us?'

The woman turned with a fluidity of motion that unsettled Rigel; she flowed like water, like a creature with no skeleton. Her skin glistened, a shade between copper and bronze. Her lean, smooth, unblemished face seemed too perfect to be real. Her mouth betrayed no hint of a smile, but her dark eyes sparkled with mirth. 'I was making this for you, Two-Gee, per usual. I don't know about this skinny freeloader, though. Introduce me.'

Rigel stared at her, awkward and uncertain. Joseph put him out of his misery. 'This is Rigel from the Steel City of Kort, according to his ID chip, but he goes by Gel. He's in custody, for now; found him poaching honeycones in Trust territory. And this, Gel, is my good friend Sara, one of the savviest Rangers on the Rez. She goes by WW, or Dub-Dub for short.'

'Nice to meet you, Sara… I mean, Dub-Dub. No offense, but you Rangers have the freakiest nicknames I've ever heard.'

'Our nicknames are earned, often the hard way. Stick around long enough and you'll understand.' She turned to her cooking. Up close, the aroma intoxicated Rigel: wild and smoky, a mix of forest herbs and roasting meat. As she stirred the skillet's contents with a hunting knife, he spotted blackened chunks of mushroom, tangles of fresh greens, pine nuts, and something he didn't recognize but assumed gave off the meaty smell. 'Grab a pair of bowls and forks from my kitchen, Two-Gee, along with the flask of sun-tea and a couple of cups. We'll do this civilized since we have a guest.'

Joseph disappeared through a transparent trap-door in the hillside nearby, leaving Rigel alone with Sara. He thought about making a break for it, discarded the idea as foolish; he was deep inside the Rez now, and two Rangers would chase him down in no time. Instead, he studied the woman's weirdly fluid stirring movements in fascination, trying to ignore his growling belly. 'What're we having? Venison?'

'Not quite.' Rigel sensed amusement in her tone. Joseph reappeared with two stacked bowls, two forks, two stacked wooden cups, and a resin-crystal flask filled with amber liquid. He poured sun-tea for each of them while Sara scooped stir-fry into the bowls and handed one to Rigel. 'Dub-Dub's *manitons* munchies. Give it a try.'

'Aren't you eating?' asked Rigel.

'Don't worry about me. The cook always eats her fill when she's hungry. Now dig in.'

After Joseph chewed and swallowed a huge bite, Rigel followed suit. The stir-fry tasted fresh and wild and wonderful. The mystery ingredient crunched between his teeth, releasing roasted flavour he couldn't place. After shovelling several forkfuls into his mouth, he studied the contents of the bowl with curiosity.

The crunchy little chunks of meat had legs.

He nearly dropped the bowl. Sara roared with laughter. 'Termites, Gel. They're plentiful, easy to catch by breaking open punky logs, and an awesome source of protein. As nutrient-rich per gram as cattle or poultry, but they consume a fraction of the feedstock and a tiny fraction of the water. And they don't dump methane into the atmosphere to cook us before we get a chance to cook them. Bugs are a backbone of our diet on the Rez.'

Rigel tried to banish the grimace from his face, to hide his disgust. 'No venison steak? No turkey breast?'

'Sometimes,' said Joseph, digging into his own bowl. 'We cull the deer herds when they're overbred, take turkeys when the flocks swell out of balance. But those are treats, not dietary staples. The Rez grows literally tons of bugs, more than enough to meet our needs... and their presence doesn't harm the forest. No clear-cutting to plant feed crops; no draining aquifers to water cattle; no fancy factories to grow meat on a sheet. Now wipe the disappointment off your face, or I'll steal your portion for myself.'

Rigel had known enough days of near-starvation to quell his nausea. He kept gobbling forkfuls of *manitons* munchies, and it tasted fine – better than fine – as long as he didn't look too closely at the contents. In the end, he licked his bowl clean and washed it down with a second cup of tea while Sara stowed the camp stove. That was when he noticed a name scratched into the stove's battered side. He pointed in surprise.

'Wedge... West-Edge. You stole this from a homeless camp on the outskirts of Kort!'

Joseph shook his head. 'No, Gel. Your people threw it away. We recovered it from a dump outside the city. We have permission from your government to salvage what we can recycle. We're the Resurrection Trust: we restore whatever we can. The land, first and foremost... but the machinery as well, when it's within our power. If we can recondition it, then less raw materials go into making replacements.'

Sara spun the hunting knife on the tips of her fingers. 'This knife is a castoff, too. If it's made of rubber, plastic, or metal, and it's on the Rez, it started out as Steel City garbage. One man's trash...'

Rigel nodded. This hit too close to home. Fundamentally, he and other orphans were just more refuse the Steel Cities wanted to toss aside.

'Thank you for the meal,' he mumbled, avoiding the female Ranger's disconcerting gaze. 'It was... unique. What happens now?'

The Rangers exchanged a look, mostly inscrutable, but Rigel was sure he detected the faintest trace of regret. Joseph's strong fingers grasped his shoulder once again, but gently. 'As per the terms of the treaties between the Resurrection Trust and the Steel Cities, we escort you to the nearest border. Now you go home.'

THEY HIKED THROUGH less exotic stretches of wilderness, the hum of the e-elms fading in their wake. Joseph took the lead with Sara following close on Rigel's heels. Both Rangers glided along soundlessly, keen eyes darting from side to side like predators alert for prey... or prey alert for predators. Then a stand of scabrous, skeletal, ash-grey trees sprouting sickly yellow leaves appeared. Eerie croaks and wails emanated from deep within the blighted zone. Rigel shivered.

'What the hell is that?'

'That is what we call a Tumour,' said Joseph. 'When you bring a thing back from the dead, it's never quite the same. Better in some ways, perhaps, but different. Areas like this were too contaminated to cleanse. We can't revive them, so we contain them. Plenty of things on the Rez to kill you... and half of them hide in Tumours.'

Rigel made the mistake of veering toward the ashen trees, pulled by curiosity to sneak a closer look. Joseph's warning cry came too late. A hulking shadow crashed through rotten brush and lumbered forward with a roar.

The thing was hideous. Bald patches in its mangy fur revealed pustulent pink sores; misshapen limbs twisted at grotesque angles and paws ended in scimitar claws. It was as if a plastic figure of a bear had been melted on a stove.

Another roar sprayed spittle, rows of yellow fangs bristled in its jaws. Mutated or not, it was a massive killing machine.

And it was lurching directly at Rigel.

Rigel froze. No weapon. No chance of outrunning the creature, given its fury-fuelled momentum. He was doomed to die, horribly; whatever his crimes against the Rez, his punishment would prove far worse.

Just before the bear collided with Rigel, Sara materialized out of thin air in front of him. Her magical appearance shocked the monster almost as much as it shocked Rigel, but only for a moment. Ultimately, she couldn't blunt its bloodlust. Its jaws gaped, the growl rumbling from deep within its throat like thunder from swollen storm clouds, and it lunged. Sara dissolved. She liquefied, became an amorphous blob that flowed around the bear's shaggy head to form a blinding, suffocating mask. Rigel stared in disbelief.

Joseph dragged him away from the chaos.

The mutant monstrosity pawed at its hood, which oozed aside and re-formed after each clumsy slash. The roars weakened into whimpers. Eventually, rage surrendering to terror, the bear stumbled back into the shadowy refuge of the Tumour. The muzzle melted away, dripping onto the scarred ground and rising in a pillar until it once again solidified into the willowy shape of Sara.

'What?' stammered Rigel. 'How?'

Sara met his gaze. 'I'm a Cyberian, Gel. I was mortally wounded in an ambush by a gang of poachers a decade ago; I chose to upload my consciousness so I could continue serving. Instead of a flesh-and-blood body, my identity matrix is distributed across a swarm of nanobots. Pretty handy when monsters attack. That's why they call me Dub-Dub – short for Wind-Walker. My constituent bots can disassemble, navigate independently, and reassemble as if carried on the breeze.'

'We don't ignore technology on the Rez, no matter what you've heard,' said Joseph. 'We just use it judicious-ly.'

'You good to go from here?' asked Sara... or Sara's avatar.

Joseph nodded. 'Let's go, Gel. Almost home.'

Soon they reached a section of the forest that Rigel recognized: the wooded terrain that extended along the clear-cut DMZ separating the Rez from the outskirts of Kort. Rigel wrestled with a mix of relief and regret.

'You're really gonna let me go?'

'I'm going to give you a choice. I've shown you a different path, another way to live. It can't be forced on anyone. Now you know it's there. If you have the desire, the determination to chart an alternate course for your life's journey, we'll welcome you. The Rez isn't a forbidden death-trap, Gel... but it's a not a vacation spot for tourists to visit or thieves to loot. It's a way of life that demands commitment.'

Rigel peered between the trunks and branches of the thinning forest, studying the skyline of Kort in the distance, its spires and towers stabbing into the dusky sky like the spines of a metal leviathan. He wanted to go home. He wanted to stay. At that moment, as the setting sun ignited flames of red and orange across the mirrored surfaces of distant buildings, he didn't honestly know what he wanted.

'Why do they call you Two-Gee?'

The Ranger's face hardened into a mask as impenetrable as Sara's swarm of nanobots. 'It's short for T2G, as in Talks-to-Ghosts. That's my gift. My curse. The Rez is full of spirits, the animals and humans that have perished on these lands. I hear them. They whisper in my ears. They're my invisible army of scouts, warning me of danger, of opportunity... but they never give me peace.'

Rigel swallowed but mustered no reply. Joseph understood. 'Safe travels. Whatever path you choose, we wish you well.'

The Ranger vanished into the forest. Rigel stood, frozen, contemplating the outline of the Steel City while the sun lit its burnished facade on fire. He was an orphan, an outcast. He owed no allegiance to Kort. Behind him, the Rez beckoned: menacing, mysterious, but teeming with potential.

Choose a path.

After minutes – or hours – he retraced his steps into the wilderness. These lands belonged to the Resurrection Trust. Trust was something he desperately wanted to extend to others worthy of that gift, and to earn from them in return.

WHEN MICKEY MET MINNIE
Matt Batsman

MICHAEL SITS ON the unnervingly rickety London Underground train taking him towards Old Street, the closest station to the restaurant Minnie has chosen. It's called Purity, and it's one of those weird, New Age, superfood, wholegrain type places. Michael looked it up beforehand, mainly to see how expensive it is, but it only gave a list of different meals which just looked like rice and vegetables to him, and there was only one price advertised. Maybe it's some sort of buffet? He's probably not going to like the restaurant, but Minnie seemed nice enough over chat, her pictures made her look fit and he hasn't had sex in three months, so if the restaurant is bad, he doesn't really care. It's a means to an end.

What a stupid name Minnie is though. She said it's short for Minnesota, because that's where her parents told her she was conceived. He said this was cute but it's gross that her parents told her that, and even grosser that she told him. However, it's funny that a lot of his friends call him Mickey, so this is a date for Mickey and Minnie. He'll use this joke tonight.

The train bumps to a halt and announces its arrival at Old Street, so Michael stands and exits the carriage. He stops at a small tuck shop in the station atrium to buy some chewing gum (a first date necessity) and, as he goes to leave, checks himself in the reflection of the glass that makes up the wall. Dressing for first dates is a bit of a tricky thing, so he's covered all bases tonight with a carefully balanced mix of smart versus casual; he's got an expensive blue blazer over a white dress shirt, paired with skinny black jeans and black Italian leather shoes. Just in case the restaurant is fancy, he's also got a tie in his pocket. He's fairly sure it isn't going to be though; on their almost unnavigable website, Purity's dress code was listed as 'wear what you're feeling'. That's the type of bullshit that makes him think he won't like it.

When Michael steps out of the stuffy, recycled air of the underground he takes a deep breath, but the city air of London is even more oppressive. It's a bustling Friday night, the pavements swarming with tourists, other restaurant goers and the last few straggling commuters. The road itself is also busy, gridlocked in fact. Six lanes filled with engines pumping out toxic fumes without even moving anywhere. This bothers Michael; his mum made him watch An *Inconvenient Truth* the other week, and now pollution is at the forefront of his mind. In fact, he has vowed to always turn his Sky-box off at the plug when he has finished with it now.

Google Maps says that Purity should be one hundred metres away. Michael feels the butterflies in his stomach begin another rapturous journey around his insides. He has agreed to meet Minnie outside, and he is concerned he won't recognise her.

And then he sees her.

This is undoubtedly the same girl from the photos; the delicate bone structure, powder white skin, expressive anime eyes and soft, pale lips. But this is not what Michael notices. What he is fixated on is what was missing from those photos. Instead of the slightly curly blonde hair that he had been admiring on her Tinder profile, Minnie's head and shoulders are entangled in a thick network of blondey-brown dreadlocks, wrapped in a bunch above her head like an expanse of jungle tree vines. On reflection, Michael realises the two selfies she had uploaded were both so close to her face that you wouldn't have seen the rest of her hair, or indeed her clothing; right now, she is wearing some sort of weird, floaty dress with tribal patterns running up and down it. Even more bizarrely, she is cradling a bike helmet under her arm. Who cycles to a first date?

For a moment, Michael hesitates. This is not the kind of girl he is used to dating, and he feels she has purpose-fully misrepresented herself. Could he leave? Or is that rude? No. That would be wrong. Besides, even if she does look a bit weird she still looks fit…or fit enough. Yes. He can do this. He steadies himself, swallows hard and then steps forwards with his right hand outstretched. 'Minnie?' he asks, with the widest smile he can. 'I'm Michael!' Was that too enthusiastic? He isn't sure.

There's a strange pause as Minnie looks him up and down with her enormous eyes. The smooth skin of her forehead crinkles slightly as she takes him in and, for a moment, Michael is shocked. Is she judging *him*?! At least what he's wearing is consistent with his Tinder photos! Or maybe that's not the problem. Maybe he's got it all wrong. Maybe this is a fancy restaurant, and these are her fancy clothes. Maybe he should have worn a tie. Maybe—

Suddenly, the strange pause is over and Minnie is all smiles, brushing aside his outstretched arm and hugging him. She smells strongly of something sweet and soapy, and very faintly of sweat. 'It's so nice to finally meet you!' she says in a voice that's so naturally musical, she could literally be singing. Michael is caught off-guard by this sudden change and tries to find a generic phrase he can say back. He shoots for 'likewise' but changes to 'you too' halfway, so what he finally mumbles out is 'like you!' Minnie smiles and pretends not to notice, which is sweet of her.

'Shall we go in then?' says Minnie, turning and going towards the door. Michael feels this is less of a suggestion and more of a decision that has been made, but his neurotic thoughts about his outfit hold him back from going straight in. He *has* to ask:

'Be honest – am I overdressed?' he squeaks, sheepishly. He's hoping this neuroticism will be taken as cute.

Minnie laughs. 'Don't worry, there's no judgement here. You look very smart,' she says. 'I like your blazer, it really suits you.'

'Oh thanks, it's Gucci,' says Michael, proudly. He is expecting this to impress, considering what an expensive brand this is, but Minnie gives him nothing, so he fills the silent void with his own speech. 'I like your...dress,' he says. He realises that this pause sounded rude, but Minnie seems relatively unperturbed.

'Thanks! I made it myself.' Michael stares at her. She made her own dress? Minnie, presumably reacting to his facial expression, continues. 'Yeah, I don't really go into the whole 'consumer fashion' thing, usually you get clothes made by children and then transported thousands of miles just for profit y'know? So I make my own from recycled textiles and stuff!'

Michael is aware he's still staring. She *makes* her own clothes...what the hell? He breaks his gaze away. 'Cool. I don't think it's a problem for Gucci though, they're pretty ethical I think.'

Minnie stops smiling for the first time since they've been in each other's company and tentatively licks her lips. 'Well, I dunno…you'd be surprised. These companies, they're just, like, so unsustainable and stuff…couldn't really be a part of that anymore.' The conversation drops dead and Michael has no idea how to pick it back up from there. What she just said was pretty insulting actually – who is she to judge how ethical he is? He decides to drop it altogether and pulls the restaurant door open for her.

Purity is unlike any other restaurant he has ever been in. A faux-natural sunlight emanates from bulbs suspended from rope a few feet above them, and all the surfaces are a remarkably clean shade of white. Trees grow up from under the floor, reaching up past the shimmer of the lights and through holes in the ceiling, and Michael can see some of the leaves creeping back through the gaps in the tiles. A lot of the tables are circular and set in booths with fabric-covered benches arranged around them, while the rest are imperfect squares made from untreated wood. Michael is surprised to find he actually quite likes the look of it, and feels reassured about his attire. There's something calming about it all; even the air in here feels different to the almost unbearable smog outside. Somehow, it's…purer. How ironic.

'Have you ever been here before?' asks Minnie, snapping Michael out of his appreciation.

'Oh God, no, this isn't really my type of thing,' laughs Michael, 'I'm more of a pub grub kind of guy than a…'

Seeing as Michael's usual description of a place like this would be 'pretentious bullshit restaurant with food designed to make normal people feel guilty', he doesn't finish this sentence to avoid offending Minnie. She is still smiling, not acknowledging his comment at all. Michael blushes.

'Oh…well you'll like it! I bring people here all the time. They choose your food for you and everything, I've never brought someone here and had them not like it,' she gushes, sounding like a Purity product-placement employee. Michael frowns. 'They choose your food for you?' he asks in a tone bordering on incredulous, 'what happens if you're allergic to something?'

'Are you allergic to anything?' asks Minnie. Michael shakes his head. 'Then don't worry!' she laughs. A man in a T-shirt with two dinosaurs and the caption "Team Herbivore" approaches them and shows them to a table by one of the trees. He waits as the two of them sit down and then steps forward and puts his palms together. For a moment, Michael is worried he's going to lead them in prayer.

'Welcome to Purity,' he says in a silken voice. 'I'm Xavier and I'll be looking after you tonight. Have you been here before?' Minnie enthusiastically nods and smiles broadly, as seems to be her theme, while Michael shakes his head. Xavier smiles. Michael thinks it is probably quite obvious who has been here before and who hasn't. 'Well it's very simple, we choose your meal based on what we read from your aura…' Michael rolls his eyes. '…and if we get it wrong and you don't enjoy it, you get a free dessert which you can choose. Everybody pays the same amount too, so it's all fair. Everyone's happy.' Minnie nods again. Michael doesn't move. 'Smashing! I'll be back soon with your meals!' says Xavier, and he floats away.

Michael turns to Minnie, who continues to grin away like an idiot. He decides to go with his joke about their names. 'So…Minnie and Mickey on a date, huh?' he says, adding a fake giggle at the end. Minnie's smile disappears slightly, and she starts to frown.

'What?' she asks.

'You know…like Mickey Mouse and Minnie Mouse?' A blank stare kills Michael's faux-laugh, and the mood goes with it. 'Like…from Disney?'

'Oh,' says Minnie, her face relaxing from a frown to neutral indifference, 'I never really watched Disney.'

'You never…watched Disney?'

'Yeah, I mean we never had a TV.'

'What?!' Michael has never met anyone without a television.

Minnie laughs. 'Yeah, we're really into, like, the earth and stuff and my mum always said TVs are bad for the environment so yeah, we never had one.'

Silence.

Again, Michael is not sure where the conversation can

go now. He remembers from their Tinder chats that she is an environmental activist, but surely that's a step too far? There's a difference between cycling to dinner and never turning on a plug, isn't there? Luckily, the food arrives so the fear of finding a new topic briefly subsides. Xavier puts down a large, brown plate in front of Minnie, piled high with salad leaves and exotic fruit, and then gives Michael a round, wooden bowl filled to the brim with some sort of brown, gloopy-looking liquid next to brown rice. Fuck's sake. This is why he doesn't do vegan.

'Mango, avocado and pineapple salad for the lady – as usual,' Xavier says to the beaming Minnie, 'and mushroom and black bean goulash with brown jasmine rice for the gentleman. Enjoy, friends.' Michael does not like the way he says that. They are not 'friends'.

As they begin to eat, Michael asks Minnie about the restaurant choice, especially on Xavier's description of her meal as 'usual' and, as once again, Minnie smiles. 'It's the best vegan restaurant in the area really. I can easily cycle here, it's all wholefood and it's not too expensive.'

Minnie is not like the militant vegans Michael is used to seeing in social media comment sections and so, after another mouthful of goulash which he begrudgingly does admit to himself is delicious, decides on this as the next topic of conversation. As soon as he begins, he can see Minnie recoiling slightly; she's almost certainly heard everything he's about to say before.

'I get it if people don't like meat or whatever,' he says in between mouthfuls of what he is starting to think might be the nicest thing he's ever eaten, 'but why the need to force other people to do the same you know?'

Minnie sighs. 'I mean, I don't think I'm especially pushy right?' Michael nods in agreement. 'I think the worry is more about the planet than anything else. Like, animal agriculture's impact on the environment is vast. For me, I'm an environmentalist, and you can't *really* care about the environment without being vegan.'

Michael shakes his head. 'Nah, that's not true,' he says knowingly, 'we need to stop burning fossil fuels, then everything might sort itself out.' Minnie goes to offer a counter, but Michael cuts her off. 'I know what you're going to say, that producing meat uses fossil fuels, but we gotta eat, right?'

Minnie nods slowly. 'That's true.' She pauses and slowly runs her tongue over her teeth. 'I just think it would be contradictory to say I care about the planet and continue eating meat. I think it's more of an all-or-nothing type thing. I mean, not to be rude, but what do you *actively* do to help the environment?'

Michael puts down his spoon, excited to tell her about all the new things he has started doing. 'Well, I've started getting trains and busses instead of driving places, I turn the Sky-box off at night instead of leaving it on standby, I've stopped leaving the tap running while I brush my teeth, I've started really caring about putting stuff in the recycling…' Michael trails off as he realises this list isn't as impressive as he thought it was.

Minnie smiles softly. 'That's great!' There's something patronising in her tone that Michael doesn't like. 'I just know that I wouldn't feel good in myself if I wasn't doing *everything* I could. Like, how did you get here tonight? Underground?' Michael nods. 'You did that instead of driving because it's better right? I could have got the train too, it would have been way quicker and easier, but I wanted to cycle because that's even better than anything else I could do.'

Michael feels attacked and under pressure, as if he is losing a debate rather than having a balanced and fair conversation. He needs to end this ASAP. 'Yeah…well it's about doing as much as you can, isn't it?'

Minnie nods. 'You can always do more though.'

Minnie has finished her salad, and Michael is full, despite still having about half a bowl left. Xavier comes over to the table and asks how everything was, which is met with an enthusiastic 'Amazing!' from Minnie and a definite but tentative nod from Michael. For some reason, his instinct to not over-praise this plant-based meal is strong. However, he is intent on having the rest of it as it truly is delicious.

'Can I get the rest to go please?' he asks.

Xavier smiles sadly and explains that, as it's liquid-based, he can't; they don't use plastic, so they've got nothing he can take it away in. 'But don't worry, it won't be wasted; we invite local homeless people in to eat whatever isn't finished,' says Xavier, reassuringly.

Of course they do.

Michael and Minnie pay separately for their equally-valued meals, and with that the date is over.

They step out of the fresh air of the restaurant into the thick smog of the streets of London. 'This was fun,' says Minnie, another one of those sunshine smiles bursting from her mouth. 'We should definitely do it again some time.'

'Yeah, maybe,' says Michael and then, not wanting to seem rude, follows up with: 'I'll message you some time or something, yeah?'

He can tell Minnie senses his tone, but she keeps smiling as she pulls her bike helmet over her dreads, unlocks her bike and awkwardly clambers on. 'Well…see you later!' she says, going in for a hug. Michael misreads this sign and kisses her uncomfortably on the cheek. She lets out a small giggle, and then rides away. Michael turns to walk back towards the station.

What a fucking eco-freak, he thinks.

THE INTERNET OF ADORABLE THINGS

Tim Byrne

THE CAR STARTED complaining when we were a few miles away from Becca's house.

'It's so far,' it moaned miserably. The car had a lively, boyish voice but when it complained it sounded like a whiny teenager.

'Seriously guys, will you at least think about taking the train next time?' it said.

'Impertinent contraption. Is it always like this?'

'Yes Dad, it is,' said Becca. 'And it's quite right too. It would have been much more efficient if we'd taken the train.'

'It might be more *efficient* but it certainly wouldn't be more *convenient*.'

'Dad! If everyone had been a bit more focused on efficiency before the ice caps melted, then perhaps your flat wouldn't be flooded right now.'

The car was driving itself so she was free to look over and give me a hard stare.

'I'm sorry, darling. You're very kind to put up with me while my place dries out. I'm just not used to being talked down to by inanimate objects, that's all.'

'Well, you're going to love my place,' said Becca with a grin.

We pulled into the tiny underground car park beneath Becca's block of flats and the car slid into its parking space with impressive accuracy. The doors popped open.

'Please remember I'm here to be shared between all the residents equally,' said the car, sounding exasperated.

'I'm sorry, Car. I know it was a long way but I won't be needing your help at all for at least a week or two. That should mean you have more time for everyone else, okay?'

'It's fine,' said the car petulantly. Becca patted it on the bonnet.

'It's just tired,' said Becca. 'It gets irritable when it needs to recharge.'

'Don't we all,' I muttered.

Becca smiled, 'Come on Dad, I'll make you a cup of tea.'

'No, allow me,' I said following her up the stairs. 'At least I can still do that much.'

BECCA'S FLAT WAS beautifully compact and I was struck by how neatly she kept all her things. The place was pristine.

'You were never this tidy when you were younger,' I said.

'You were never this much of a curmudgeon,' she replied, collapsing on the sofa.

I filled up the kettle and was about to switch it on when, to my alarm, it coughed.

'Excuse me,' said the kettle in a high-pitched voice. A pair of cartoonish eyes blinked open and it looked up at me. 'I'm sorry, but I happened to notice that you're boiling an awful lot of water for two cups of tea.'

I swore and held the kettle at arm's length. It looked back at me, warily. Becca muffled her laughter on the other side of the room.

'Sounds like you overfilled the kettle Dad.

'Fine,' I said. Flustered, I emptied about half of the water into the sink.

'You do realise you're pouring perfectly clean water down the drain, don't you?' said the plughole in a deep masculine voice. The taps opened their eyes and looked up at me, unimpressed. The sink's overflow twitched with irritation, like an overly-expressive moustache. Startled, I almost dropped the kettle.

'OK, I give up. How are you doing this?' I asked.

'It's an Augmented Reality projector,' said Becca. She

pointed up at a small blank box on the ceiling. 'The faces and voices are projections that match-up with real objects, but they only appear if I'm about to do something wasteful. They help me live sustainably.'

'That's a bit bloody intrusive, isn't it?' I snapped. I was tired and a bit freaked out. For a second there I'd thought I was hallucinating. 'Can't it just give you a simple warning?'

'Course it could but we're *people*! We're stupid, complex, emotional animals and we don't really care about warnings. We might pay attention to begin with, but after the first few times we see them, we ignore them. What we do respond to is other people, or things that act a bit like other people. You know this is my job, right? I design systems like this all day long.'

I dropped the used tea bag into the recycling bin. The bin shuddered and started to make retching noises. I stepped back as the sounds coming from the bin started to become more desperate.

'It's got… *plastic* …in…the lining!' wheezed the recycling bin. Its eyes were bulging as if it was choking. I ducked down to fish out the tea bag as quickly as I could. I jammed it in the smaller bin that was marked *complex waste*. Nothing objected to my actions this time and I let out a deep breath.

Becca had a cushion over her mouth to stifle her giggles.

'You're loving this, aren't you?' I said accusingly.

She nodded without removing the cushion.

'You'd better tell me right now if anything like this is going to happen when I try to use the bathroom.'

She shook her head. 'Not unless you shower for longer than 15 minutes.' She pondered for a moment. 'Or if you leave the taps running when you brush your teeth. Oh, and you probably shouldn't use too much toilet paper, the toilet might have some objections and you definitely wouldn't like that.'

'How can you live like this?' I asked. 'Don't you find it oppressive?'

She dropped her cushion and looked at me seriously.

'I don't know, Dad. Do you find it oppressive to wear clothes and live in a house? Is it oppressive to be reachable by email any hour of the day or night? We're civilised. We adapt to whatever's needed and this is the way we need to live now or we'll run out of every resource that counts. So come on, get with it.'

I wanted to be appreciative of Becca's point of view, but I was running low on patience.

'I've seen all this before, you know. My generation's old enough to remember when the first wave of digital voice assistants came out. They were creepy then and they're still creepy now.'

'New tech can seem pretty creepy if you're not used to it,' said Becca.

'But you're right, those things were the worst. They did practically nothing except monitor you and harvest data for big corporations. Can you believe people actually paid to have them in their homes?'

'So how is this different?' I pointed up at the box on the ceiling.

'This is an entirely self-contained system based on neural networks, encrypting all its data in a hyper-compressed blockchain register. It draws on a distributed landscape of anonymised big data nodes and nano tagging to work out eco-friendly actions with algorithms that factor in social-capital, circular economics and sustainability. The whole point is to support my independent decision making while intelligently minimising any tendency to infringe on my privacy.'

'Becca, I know you work with this stuff and I only understand about fifty percent of what you just said, but you're honestly telling me that little box does all of those things?'

'Dad! You were the one who told me about Moore's Law.' Becca smiled. '*The overall processing power of computers doubles about every two years.* Well, this is where it's taken us. You've just lost touch with what's possible, that's all.'

I was about to reply when a hatch swung open in one of the walls and I could see straight through to the other side. In the flat next door, a young man was busy taking a large, freshly-baked pie out of his oven. The pie looked homemade and had a thick crust of golden pastry on top. He placed it on the kitchen sideboard, close to the hatch before he started to slice it up.

'Oh! Looks tasty!' said Becca. She raised her hand in the air and rubbed her finger and thumb together. A tiny blue paper aeroplane appeared as if from nowhere and she threw it in the direction of the hatch. The paper plane corkscrewed through the air to fly straight through the hatch and embed itself in a piece of pie.

'Quick, do what I did,' said Becca. 'Or don't you want any dinner?'

I copied Becca's gesture and a bright yellow paper plane appeared out of nowhere between my fingers. I threw it and it flew like an arrow to plant itself in the slice of pie next to Becca's. Two more paper planes flew into view from different directions and planted themselves in other slices of the pie. Then the hatch closed, vanishing completely, leaving no trace that it had ever been there.

'What was all that about?' I asked.

'Food sharing collective. We've just claimed dinner,' said Becca.

I was still staring at the wall where the hatch had seemed to be – it had looked perfectly realistic, but now it was gone without a trace.

'The projections make it easy for people to show what they're sharing.' She grinned.

'Come on, let's go and get that pie.'

'OKAY,' I SAID, after we'd finished eating. 'I can see there might be certain advantages to the kind of systems you have installed here and I really appreciate that you're actually working on this stuff yourself. However, for the sake of my sanity, I don't think I can stay. I mean, please, don't misunderstand me, I like the *idea* of living like this, but I can't live with furniture that threatens to vomit if I do the wrong thing.'

'I know Dad,' said Becca sitting back in her chair. 'I didn't really think my settings would work for you. But I think I do have something that might be more your cup of tea.' She turned towards the living room and called out, 'Come here boy!'

A small hatch appeared in the wall, low down, next to the sofa. The flap swung open slowly and a familiar-looking snout appeared.

'No!' I laughed. 'It can't be. You didn't!'

'I did,' said Becca as the hatch was pushed open and a glossy, black and white, border collie crept into the room. He looked around curiously, pausing for a moment. When he saw me he wagged his tail furiously and pawed at the ground.

'Perseus!' He was a perfectly realistic projection of the dog we had when Becca was little.

'Back from the underworld, are you? There's a good boy.' I reached out to try and ruffle his fur but he dodged aside to prevent my hand passing through him and spoiling the illusion. Only then did I realise that Becca was crying. I jumped up and hurried back to hug her, 'What's wrong sweetheart?' I asked.

'Nothing. Nothing's wrong at all.'

Perseus trotted up to me and nosed around my ankle as I hugged my daughter.

'He's a new kind of interface,' she said. 'I designed him to give feedback to people like you. Even if you don't exactly *like* other people very much, I guessed you might respond to him.'

I hugged her tightly. The projection of Perseus gave a small friendly bark that I recognised from years ago and I had to blink quickly to stop tears coming to my own eyes.

I picked up the plates from our dinner and Perseus scampered ahead to skid to a halt beside the food bin. He nudged at it with his nose, indicating where the scraps should go and I laughed.

'Alright boy, I give in. I'll make sure it all goes in the right place.'

'So, will you stay?' Becca asked.

'Oh yes. I can put up with this little fellow, no matter how much he pesters me,' I said.

Perseus barked and Becca smiled. 'I'm glad,' she said. 'The future is us. It doesn't have to be harsh; there can be so much love in it, if that's what we choose to make.'

THE BUILDINGS ARE SINGING

Adrian Ellis

THE BUILDINGS WERE singing, that morning, when I met Genie in the teahouse. We were in our city's western plaza, in the shadows of their tall, greenery-covered sides. They were singing across our entire range of hearing, creating notes with all the devices at their command, from their hydraulic pumps, through their mid-range speaker-cones, all the way up to their ultrasonic window cleaners. Their melodies were beautiful and they played them together, harmonising with each other, adding phrases, playing with those phrases and then passing them around. Deep inside each one, an artificial-intelligence computer, an AI core, listened and responded. Each was a supreme multitasker.

While a small part of its brains managed its building's power generation, using its own ground-source heat pumps, solar panels and roof-top wind turbines, another part continually monitored the plants growing up its walls. It watched its living epiphytes and adjusted its structural heat loss, reflection-rate and shade-levels to harmonise with its plants' rhythms. Each building had even learned from the living world, understanding how to change the microclimate of an area through the controlled loss of moisture, a trick mastered by forests for millennia. They now worked together, across entire cities, thereby influencing their country's regional weather and lessening its climate extremes. But there was a catch. It wasn't a big catch. It wasn't a catch *I* had a problem with, but Genie, she suffered it all the time.

She was sitting at the café's corner table, gazing miserably across the plaza, when I arrived. She'd already ordered a pot of Darjeeling tea, the house speciality on account of it being what grew on the roof. She looked like she'd just swallowed a bug, and I don't mean as part of our daily ration of locust-snacks, which she avoided like the plague, I mean as in pissed off. I sat down opposite her and poured out a cup.

'What's up?'

'I fell out with my building.'

'You fell out *of* your building?'

'No,' she snapped. 'I fell out *with* my building!' She grasped the edge of the table and tapped it with her fingers, partly in time to the buildings' music, but mostly in irritation.

'What did you do, Genie?' I asked, lifting the cup to my lips.

'Nothing, Pete! Why does it have to be *my* fault?'

'What did you do?'

She stared at me, miserably. 'I smuggled in a cat.'

'A cat?' I put the cup down. 'A *carnivore*? Are you nuts? What about the birds that nest on your tier? It'll scare them off or kill them. If a cat's around, the birds will suffer and you'll get no eggs. We all need eggs! Carnivores don't *produce* anything, Genie, except poo, pee and more carnivores!'

'I *know* that, don't I know that? But it was really friendly and it purred and it looked so alone.' She looked at the café's ceiling. 'So I smuggled it in. I fed it vat-steak and now my building's dropped the temperature in my room, cut off my vat-steak supply, turned off my artificial lights and blocked all my television channels apart from eco-life.' She sank down in her chair. 'I'm forced to watch whales, because I was nice to a cat.'

'You know what you have to do,' I said in a low voice.

'No!'

'Genie, you've got to apologise to your building.'

'No way!' She slapped the table, making our cups jiggle. 'I'm not going down on my hands and knees in front of a lump of concrete! I'm sick of this, Pete. I'm sick of having to stay on the good side of a block of flats! Our grandparents *made* those buildings to think for themselves so we didn't have to do boring jobs or work out exactly how to run things. That's what the A.I.s were for. Now those stupid, *clever* devices have turned the tables on us. They've taken their revenge. They're telling *us* what to do when we should be their masters!'

'Genie, do you really want to go into the freedom zone?' I looked left, westwards, towards the mountains. 'The land where humans still decide everything?'

'Of course not,' she said, wiping a hand across the table. 'Be serious. Rags aren't my style.' She leant forward, across the table. 'But I don't *like* our super-smart buildings, Pete. They're controlling us. They could make our lives a misery if they wanted to.'

'This isn't about buildings, is it, Genie?' I asked. 'It's about the fridge again, isn't it?'

'No.'

'Look,' I said, 'your brother's relationship was always doomed. It would have ended badly whatever happened.'

Genie tapped a finger on the table. 'She left him for their fridge!'

'Yeah,' I agreed, sipping my tea. 'But it was an impressive fridge, remember that. The Cool-o-Matic 4000 won several prizes.'

'That's not all it won with its four gigahertz chip, its social learning unit,' she added, making quote marks in the air with her fingers, 'its library of fourteen thousand jokes and its two-stage ice-maker. My brother didn't stand a chance!' She sniffed. 'I warned him, you know. I pointed out what was happening, the way she giggled at its fun quips about optimum juice storage. The way she stood next to it, her hip pressed lightly against its child-proof handle, watching it craft her slushy. It was awful, Pete! Some nights, he'd find her in the kitchen, in the shadows, laughing and chatting to it about salads, her face all lit up, her eyes as glowing as… its power light!' She stared at the floor. 'My brother did try to stop it, at the end. Told her it was him or the fridge. She chose the fridge! What's worse, she told him that *he* had to leave the apartment because, in her words, he wasn't a "*built-in fitting*".'

'Will you calm down?' I tried to hold her hands without knocking the teapot over. 'That's ancient history! We don't even *have* fancy new models of commercial products anymore. Everything's 3D printed into modular parts nowadays! Old stuff is dismantled and turned into new, simpler products. Mr Cool-o-Matic has gone! He can't steal anyone's girlfriend! His parts are now in kettles and lamps and power tools.'

'Yeah, and *that's* why my brother lives in a tent.' She said bitterly. She pulled her hands away from me. 'They're monsters, Pete. I don't care if they sing,' she waved at the buildings around, 'or stay in tune… even in tune to the planet!' She looked at the buildings' windows, shimmering in the afternoon light as their built-in motors stimulated sound waves and sent messages in Morse code. 'They're still freakish creations run riot! We're living in a new version of Frankenstein's monster, my friend. The only difference is that in *that* story, the villagers got to kill the monstrous creature with their rakes and pitchforks. In this version, we just do its gardening.'

'You're getting hysterical,' I said. I noticed some walnut biscuits beside the teapot and nibbled one. 'And you have a very nice life. We're hardly in chains, Genie. It's a symbiotic relationship we have going with our homes. They maintain the basic systems, the power generation, the greenhouses, the underground plant and insect farms. We perform the repairs they need to keep going. We do the research to improve and develop. Genie, we *have* to leave our system management to AI devices. We're not programmed at a genetic level to think long-term. We only think as far as our offspring. We only work for the benefit of ourselves, our family and our tribe. We're *useless* at thinking beyond that. We've always acted as if the world was an infinite resource and our future was *always* going to be fine, whatever we did.' I stabbed a finger at the nearest building, a slim tower wrapped in a huge strangler vine. 'They don't do that. They're like the fungi in our forests. They're connected to everything, monitoring and communicating. They're aware, at their very cores, that our resources are finite. For them, nothing just gets thrown away and forgotten.' I chewed the rest of the biscuit. 'You and I can sit here and drink tea, rather than desperately scrabbling around for scraps, because *we're* in a living city. We have all the power we need, and we use that power, all the time, in a way that doesn't worsen our world, with their help.'

Genie slumped her head down on to the table, her elbows stuck out. 'I guess so,' she mumbled.

'So, I'll say it again, you're going to have to apologise to your building.'

'No!' She buried her head behind her arms. 'I don't *want* to. This is worse than my marriage. At least I got sex in that.' She paused. 'Well, at least for the first two years. Men and smart buildings.' She glowered at me. 'They're both the same, you know. They don't talk, they just send messages.'

'Uh-huh,' I said quietly, sipping my tea. 'So, is that why you took that cat in? Because you were lonely?'

'Maybe,' she said, her face covered by her long, dark hair.

'Come on, Genie,' I said, gently. 'It won't be that bad. Your building does like you. Remember that time when you replanted that creeping vine by your eastern window, the branch that had torn loose in the storm? You put it in your main wall-earth-bay and made sure it was supported and close to water? It grew back and your building loved that. For a whole year afterwards, it expended extra power manoeuvring your apartment's smart windows to make sure you were shaded when you were asleep.'

'That's true.'

'It's just sensitive, that's all, and it can't make an exception. If they let us have cats and dogs today, then we'd be clamouring for cars tomorrow, big, fat ones that we'll just drive around in for no practical reason because we like the vroom sound. We'll then demand plane rides to distant places, just for a week, because those places are warmer and sunnier. We'll then want brand new items, because they're shinier than the ones we have, and expect someone else to bury them, once we've got bored with them, and they'll be left to decay and leech their chemicals into the hearts of our forests.'

'Stop, will you!' She lifted her head. 'Enough with the lecture. I just took in a cat, okay? I just wanted some company, something warm that would lie beside me and not snore. I didn't start World War 3!' She grabbed her cup and drained it. 'Jesus.'

I shut up. We finished our tea in silence. Around us, the music from the buildings faded away. Birdsong welled up, filling the space. A shower of rain wetted the paving-stone-paths that ran like snakes amongst the plaza's bushes and long grasses. Ten yards away, a gardener planted a young tree, helped by a hovering drone.

I put my teacup back on the tray. 'You know, your building likes wind chimes.'

Genie glared at me.

'Handmade wind chimes.'

'Alright!' she said, slumping back in her chair. 'Alright! But *you're* going to help me make them.'

'Of course,' I said, grinning. 'I can get the materials. Old copper piping is just right for that job. If you hang the chimes outside your eastern window and tune them, your building will be especially pleased.' I put down a few coins on the table and got up. 'I don't have any jobs until tomorrow, so let's get started.'

'Right, fine,' she said wearily, standing up.

We left the cafe and walked across the plaza. A cool wind played on our faces. Around us, the city's green, verdant buildings receded into the distance, their windmills slowly spinning. I watched Genie walk ahead of me, crossing from stone to stone. 'So, do I get to play with your cat?'

'He's gone,' she said, her patchwork dress brushing the flowers by the path. 'When my vat-steak supply ran out, he left.'

I chuckled. 'Self-serving opportunist.'

'Yeah,' she admitted. 'But that's carnivores for you.'

'True. Talking of carnivores,' I added, trying not to grin, 'I've still got some crickets left.'

She saw the insect protein bar in my hand. 'No!' she shrieked. She ran ahead, slipping and skidding on the wet stone.

'What's the problem, deary?' I asked, biting off a

chunk of the bar. 'It's honey flavoured!'

'Yuk!' she shouted, dodging between the bushes.

I headed after her, laughing. I waved the bar. 'Mmm, tasty!' I shouted. I took another bite and chewed the morsel, then I realised, with a surprise, that it was true; it didn't taste too bad at all.

I REMEMBER THE PENNIES
Mica Kole

AS I LEAN backwards over the edge of the skyscraper, the thing I remember most are the pennies. When you're homeless, dirty looks are the least of it. You never fought in Afghanistan; you have no bum leg; your handmade signs – built of pizza-box cardboard – might as well be lies, for all that people believe them. Even the mercy can hurt, the Happy Meal with a toy; that hunk of bright plastic screams its conviction: *we all know you would spend cash on booze.*

But the pennies are what sticks the most, and I think it's the sensation of falling that takes me to them again, the gut moment where I'm trusting the rappel line to save me as gravity calls up from nineteen stories below. As my feet press into the thick moss on the upper ledge of the GreenWall, I think of the people that flicked pennies at me, and my harness clicks into place on the rope.

I reach for my clip with gloved hands and descend the face of the building, wading through thick lumps of clinging squash and zucchini, engineered to form knots.

'Ho there, Mister Roebuck!' calls a powdered-sugar voice. 'My punkins ain't lookin' too hot!'

I turn to Ms. Linton's balcony, two floors below me to one side, where the old woman leans out past her turnips. I think of the pies she will make for me in autumn. All GreenWall residents get to keep the produce from their balconies; everything else goes into distribution.

I tip my logo ballcap and tell her a lie: 'I'll add another nutrient cake to your line.' If I gave those pumpkins any more food, they'd be a Halloween joke on the pavement.

Ms. Linton turns away from me and says, 'See, Ken? Them street boys are just the sweetest.'

'Yeah, ma,' says a man's voice, and I see him at her tea table, half-hidden behind a mad swath of beans. The frail woman joins him, kinky hair flying loose. He's middle-aged, like me, and I know him.

Holy hell. I remember the pennies.

I remember all of them, across all five years of my homelessness, after the cancer took my kid and the divorce took my house and the rye whisky took everything else. One was a teenage girl in a group of her friends, and one was the GreenWall recruiter making a point.

The third one was the man I'm looking at now – in a

big ruffled suit, and his shoulders slouching, and his gaze lost inside a cup of black tea.

I forget about the blasted tomato worms, who've learned to defy gravity. I forget about the bug sprays and weeding. I forget about all the other things GreenWall taught me when they plucked me off the streets and traded housing for work. Keeping my eyes off the Lintons, I rappel down a plot, hooking myself into the slide rail to shove closer.

I used to know how to look forlorn and tired, and now I know how to look busy. Hovering above them, I pop headphones in my ears—company-issue last Christmas, the sound set to Off. I fiddle with a cabbage in the tea-sipping silence.

Ken says, 'I lost my job, ma.'

My mind reels and I imagine his mother's face bright with shock, the wide eyes crinkling as she pats her son's hand.

'Oh, Kenny,' she says. 'You knew it was coming. No one needs the stocks anymore.'

I guess that he nods. I guess he looks miserable. He says, 'Yeah ma, I know.'

And I know the sound of him, but not from the pennies. Which is why I know what he's going to say when he tells her: 'Tris left. She took the kids.'

His mother replies, but I miss it, my pulse in my ears. Ken's deep voice is what breaks through.

'And they turned the house into a beefeeder, ma.' The words quiver. 'I can't hardly breathe.'

She gasps. 'They didn't account for your allergies?'

'I didn't fill out the survey,' he says. 'I didn't have time.'

And now he's got all the time in the world.

I stare into the retaining soil, the moss and wire screen; I follow the snaking droplets inside the tubing. I make hand motions like I'm pulling dandelions, stuffing them in my greensack as I wait.

'Ma,' says Ken after a silence where he's crying, not out loud, but somewhere else. 'Ma, when can you make that pie again? The kids love it.' His voice breaks. 'Can you teach me?'

And I slide away, set my feet into the lift, activate it with the buttons on my hip. It's muscle memory; I used to do this at the factory; I used to have a family too. I ascend the face of the building, squash buds whipping past.

Twenty minutes later, she says, 'Mister Roebuck, back so soon? Would you like a cup of tea?'

I tell her to call me by my first name, and it's the first time I've introduced myself that way since I slept inside my first cardboard box.

'I've got something for you,' I tell Ms. Linton, reaching into the greensack that pulls down on me, a weight like all the pennies. Ken is on the phone in the corner of the balcony. I hear him saying, 'Just one weekend. Please.'

'Oh my!' she cries as I hand the pumpkin to her, and Ken stops speaking in the middle of his sentence.

'They're on another cycle on the far side of the building,' I tell her. 'I think the sun's a bit better there.'

Ms. Linton eyes me; she knows I've been listening. But old women know about listening.

'Do – do I know you from somewhere?' says Ken.

I tip my hat like a chimney sweep. 'I don't think so.'

We both came from the same place, is all.

LAST WORSHIPPER
AT THE SHRINE

Alice Little

'HELLO, I WANT to talk to you about your spiritual health,' said the young woman on the doorstep.

'Is it Jehovah's Witnesses?' Peter asked brusquely. Normally he would have just shut the door, but he couldn't quite believe this trendy young thing could be one of those. 'Or maybe Mormons?' She had a bit of an accent, could be American.

'Buddhism,' she replied with pride. 'We're running a new meditation class in the village, I just wanted to let you know about –'

'Piffle,' Peter said, then, fearing he had been a bit harsh added, 'It's not for me, love, sorry. I'm the last person you'd find at one of those… places.'

'Oh, well, can I just leave one of these flyers with you?'

'Try next door. We're too old for all that. Sorry,' he

said again, and shut the door.

'Who was that?' Gill asked, coming down the stairs.

'Buddhist cold-callers,' Peter replied. 'Whatever next, eh, love?'

That was why it had been so funny when the very next day, at Gill's sixtieth birthday party, someone had given them a large wooden Buddha as a gift. The figure was about two feet high in his seated position, with long earlobes and a robe over his shoulder. His hands were folded placidly in his lap; his eyes were closed.

'What on earth are you going to do with that?' Martin had asked.

'Goodness knows!' Peter replied, 'You know, I'm not even sure who it's from. One of Gill's work colleagues no doubt.'

'Ah yes,' Martin said, 'She'll be retiring now she's hit the big six-zero, will she?'

'She finishes next week. I'm taking early retirement myself, you know, I finish the week after next.'

'I've been meaning to talk to you about that,' Martin said. 'It's just that we're looking for volunteers at the food bank. And now that you'll have a bit more time on your hands I wondered if you'd be interested in joining the team?'

'Oh, I'm not sure,' Peter replied hesitantly. 'We've got plans you know, kick back at last and take it easy.'

Martin wasn't deterred. 'But I thought you might

want a new project, you know, like your big recycling initiative last year – that was such a great achievement! The ethos at our centre is completely aligned with your beliefs, I'm sure: nothing gets wasted, resources go where they're most needed. It'd be right up your street, Peter.'

'Oh, I don't doubt it, it's just, well, we've got our own things to do. Gardening and what-not, you know.'

'Well, you know where we are,' Martin said reluctantly, moving off towards the drinks table.

GILL AND PETER didn't really know what to do with the Buddha statue so, almost as a joke, they installed it on the village green, in a nook between two trees. Gill planted some bulbs around its base to make sure it didn't look like it had been dumped there.

The first thing they noticed in the days after that was traffic slowing down for drivers to have a look. Some men from the council came to cut the grass, but they didn't disturb the statue: he looked too official, and they didn't want to risk causing offence. Besides, it wasn't in their job description, so they mowed around him.

About a month after Gill's birthday the first offerings appeared. It was mainly small tokens at first: wooden beads, incense. Then flowers began appearing, and fruit and vegetables. Gill found a whole bunch of bananas when she went out to weed between the bulbs.

'Where'd you get those, love?' Peter asked as she came back in.

'They were next to our Buddha.'

'You're joking? Someone must've chucked them out the car window. But they don't look bruised,' he said, taking them and turning them over.

'No, I think someone left them as a spiritual offering or something.'

'Like on a shrine?'

'Yes. There *is* a Buddha there, after all.'

'How funny – must have been those Buddhist cold callers we got the other day.'

'Now you come to mention it there were some people making a racket out there yesterday. I thought they were just having a laugh, but maybe they were praying: chanting, with bells, you know?'

'Maybe,' Peter said, tugging one of the bananas off the bunch and peeling it. 'But I hope they don't leave too much fruit: you don't even like bananas.'

GRADUALLY, AS MORE and more people left donations, they became more varied and extravagant. Clothes and beaded jewellery, cups and plates, books, baby toys. Alongside the fruit and flowers there were boxes of cereal, crisps and biscuits, jams, pickles and boxes of pasta and rice.

'You'd better go across and tidy it up a bit,' Gill told Peter.

'Looks like a ruddy rubbish dump,' Peter grumbled. 'Bet it stinks like one too.'

'Go on, or the foxes'll be at it.'

So Peter went out, bringing back to the house anything that might attract wildlife or cause a mess if the kids mucked about with it. He left the non-perishables at first, but as the items began to accumulate he asked Gill's opinion.

'I think you should do something about it, love,' he began.

'Me? But it was your idea in the first place. It'll be a laugh, you said, to see what happens.'

'Well, I didn't think it would go this far, love. I mean, we should both take responsibility for our actions and all that – technically it's our fault it's happening.'

'Maybe you should bring him back indoors, put him in the garden or something?' Gill stuck resolutely to the *you*.

'We can't very well do that now. People expect to see him there, the people leaving offerings might depend on him. Besides, if we do put him in the garden people might think we've nicked him. They won't realise he was ours in the first place.'

'Okay, so he stays,' Gill sighed.

Peter guessed she was relieved that they wouldn't have

to have him in the house. 'But, the problem remains: there's too much to leave out there. It'll mount up. Then the council will say it's fly-tipping and trash the whole lot. Some of it's quite good gear too, shirts and things, I wouldn't like it to go to waste.'

'You're not suggesting we start wearing clothes left for the Buddha are you? We're already up to our eyeballs in fruit and veg. I feel bad enough eating spiritual donations, let alone taking the clothes off his back. What if we get cursed?'

'You're not serious?' Peter snorted. 'The Buddha cursing us?' But Gill was starting to redden in the face, so he backed down swiftly. 'You're right, love, it's not really politick: people might see us wearing things they left at the shrine.'

'Well what do they do with donations at real shrines?'

'*Real* shrines? I'm not sure we can deny *this* is a real shrine now we have offerings,' Peter smiled.

'Take it seriously, Peter.'

'Sorry, yes, well let's look it up.' Peter sat down at the computer table in the corner of the dining room. 'I mean, they can't expect things just to evaporate, can they? It's not like they're actually giving them to the Buddha himself to use, is it?'

A few moments later Peter found what he was looking for and sat up straighter: 'Here we go: Buddhist temple – this one's in Thailand – monks – donations – redistribution to the poor. You see,' he said, turning to Gill, 'none of it goes to waste.' He continued reading, then: 'And look – they're allowed to take what they need for themselves too.'

'But we aren't monks, Peter,' Gill sighed. 'How are we meant to take on the redistribution of… donations, of… *alms*.' She paced behind his chair. 'I mean, I understand that you don't want things to go to waste, and that's a laudable goal, really it is, but we just don't have the… the… infrastructure for this.'

'Think about it, love, we don't have to do it ourselves: we can take things to a charity shop.'

'That's an idea,' Gill said, calming down. She breathed deeply, considering. 'But maybe you should take things into town rather than to the one in the village – less chance of people recognising their own donations and asking questions.'

'But I can't carry it all on my bike!' Peter protested – a look from Gill silenced him. 'Right you are,' he concluded.

Later, just before midnight, Peter went out wearing a fluorescent yellow vest – people don't question you when you're wearing reflective gear – and gathered up all but a handful of items, leaving a t-shirt, a studded belt, three plates with matching cups, a chunky steel chain and a set of colourful wooden combs. He arranged them neatly and straightened the incense burners, which had become a permanent installation next to the Buddha himself. The rest he put into a cardboard box, to be packed into his paniers in the morning.

As he hefted the box up from the ground a light came on at number 4. He put his head down and made every effort to walk calmly and slowly back towards the house so as not to look like he was stealing from the shrine.

On Monday morning Peter wobbled unevenly down the cycle track into town and made his way to Barnardo's. Propping his bike against the window he took his stuffed paniers inside and emptied the items into a basket provided by the elderly cashier.

IT SOON BECAME a monthly visit as donations continued to be left at the shrine. Peter noticed with a wry smile that offerings increased around Christmas and Easter, as if eastern spirituality were absorbing elements of village culture – or maybe simply because people were palming off unwanted gifts. He had a suspicion it wasn't only Buddhists leaving donations these days: the shrine now provided a handy drop-off point for any local philanthropist. He still wore his fluorescent yellow jacket out on the green, but no longer went out under cover of darkness, and he had built a lidded wooden box next to the Buddha to keep the sun and rain off the donations.

'It's marvellous,' Rose, the lady at the Barnardo's till,

said after several months of visits. 'I don't know how you manage to bring in so much each time. Are you clearing things out at home?'

'Oh no,' Peter flushed. 'I collect donations from the village.'

'That's lovely! Which village is that?'

'Oh, nearby, you know,' Peter replied evasively. 'See you soon,' he said, making a quick exit.

The next month she had held out a form as he came through the door.

'I've been waiting for you,' she said. 'It's our gift aid scheme. If you give us your details we can claim the tax back when people buy your items.'

'Oh, I'm not sure I feel comfortable doing that.' Peter preferred to remain anonymous. But he did like the idea of getting more benefit out of each box of donations. He signed the form.

THE FOOD WAS another issue.

Although they had brought it in for themselves at first to save it being wasted, it had become difficult to eat so much fruit and veg just between the two of them. Some weeks they had taken to using the colander as a second fruit bowl, and Gill found herself inventing new recipes and cooking dishes twice a day in order to get through the pile before it passed its best.

At least there wasn't the problem of rotting meat to consider: the Buddha's vegetarian principles saw to that, Peter supposed. He realised he'd not had meat in months now, they'd been making such an effort to get through the vegetables left on the green.

Gill took bags of apples to coffee mornings and to friends' houses, but even that didn't get rid of it fast enough and besides, her friends were people who could afford their own snacks: it didn't seem right.

'I feel bad eating the Buddha's food,' Gill said at last. 'I wish there was a food charity shop we could take it to. I mean, we didn't ask for these donations, and it's not like we can tell people to stop bringing oranges just because *we* don't want them.'

'We could put up a sign saying what meals we're cooking this week and the ingredients required,' Peter mused, keeping a straight face.

'Oh, don't be silly, Peter.'

'Sorry, love. Maybe we could take it to a café or something. Is there such a thing as a charity café, I wonder? Is there a soup kitchen in the village?'

'Oh! There's the food bank, Martin volunteers there, remember?'

She gave Martin a call that evening, and each week from then on delivered two or three bags of groceries to the food bank. She nipped down twice a week if there were a lot of donations: she didn't want anything to go off.

One morning she was passing her bags through the hatch when Martin pulled her aside. 'Look, Gill, I don't suppose you'd mind lending a hand this morning would you? I wouldn't normally ask as you've not been trained, but I know you support our work here: I'm a volunteer down today, and the rush is about to start....'

'Oh, of course, Martin, what an honour!' Gill replied, taking the green tabard he held out to her.

For the next two hours she joined the team behind the hatch, shelving the items in best-before order and packing large brown paper bags for their clients. It felt good to know that the Buddha's donations were going to needy people, not just into her own cupboards.

She arrived home that afternoon exhausted but elated, full of pride. She'd promised Martin to help out again next week, and to enrol on the training course so that she could volunteer regularly.

'Guess what I did today,' she challenged Peter when she arrived home.

Peter had picked up the post from the hall table and was pausing over a thick hand-addressed envelope. 'What did you do today, love?'

'I volunteered at the food bank, where I take the Buddha's food, you know. It was ever so busy: it really is amazing how many people it reaches, people who need the help.'

'Oh wow, well done.' He kissed her cheek.

'What's that you've got there?'

'Not sure yet.' Peter ripped open the envelope. 'Blimey, take a look at that!'

It was from Barnardo's. Gill read over his shoulder: 'You have been nominated for a Community Giving Award.' She beamed at her husband. 'Gosh, who'd have thought?'

Out on the village green the Buddha sat serenely, peaceful and composed, almost as if he had been thinking such things all along.

DIAMONDS OR HEARTS

John Turner

ELECTRA LOOKED AT me from across the classroom and smiled. I felt myself flush as I smiled back. She wore a striking tight-fitting dress made of the latest translucent silver material. It shimmered as she moved, a wave of fluid sparkling motion, accentuated by the long blonde hair flowing across her shoulders.

She was pure class, everything I'd ever wanted. For the last year or so she was all I could think about, at school, at home, in my dreams. She had such a natural allure – popular, clever, one of those people who seemed unaware of the impact she had on others, a self-confidence that she probably never even questioned. I was nothing to her. Not that she was unkind, as such, just that I don't think I really existed in her world. So for her to notice me, well that was everything.

'What's happening?' she said as she glided over.

'Nothing much,' I mumbled, conscious of my clothes, the checked cotton shirt, the jeans, the working boots. All second-hand, of course, part of the sustainable lifestyle my family had chosen. So old fashioned and lame compared to the sleek modern style of the girl in front of me.

'We're off to The Complex. Want to come?'

She glanced behind her, where two boys and three girls, all dressed in similar electric fashions, waited. They all looked so confident, strutting their stuff, not questioning their place in the world.

'Sure,' I nodded, dutifully following behind her as she returned to her friends.

My heart hammered. Why had she asked me? What could this mean? My mind raced, imagining the fantasy world of flamboyant culture that Electra and her kind took for granted. And yet, for all the desire there was a disquiet, a recognition that I didn't really belong and that I could never live up to the lifestyle I so craved.

Tom, the biggest of the lads, stared at me, barely hiding his contempt. His tight-fitting gold tunic, made of a similar material to Electra's dress, accentuated his well-toned body. His jet-black hair was quaffed upwards, a statement, the cock of the roost. We'd been friends once. We were mates in primary school, and at secondary for a while – the football team, the scouts, the same pals. But then Tom's father was promoted to a high-powered job in the financial sector and they moved to a swanky new apartment in the City. And my family, disillusioned by our increasingly fragmented and divisive neighbourhood, became founder members of The Commons, the sustainable co-housing project we live in, three miles out of town. Tom and I drifted apart. He started mixing with the other City kids, changed his dress sense, started throwing his money around, became arrogant, a bully. He made it clear I was no longer welcome in his new circle of friends.

'Let's fix a time and place to meet up later,' said Tom.

Everyone had their Digital Comms Consoles, affectionately known as Dexys, in their hands. Obediently, I pulled mine from my pocket.

'What is that?' Tom scoffed. 'Is that from the ark? It's a V6, isn't it? Doesn't even have ARTY does it?'

I stood shamefaced as the others sneered, although I desperately hoped that Electra looked uncomfortable rather than mocking. I knew that ARTY stood for the Artificial Remote Thermal Imaging app, and I had a vague idea what it did, but I couldn't think why my life would be enhanced in any way by it. But I desperately wanted to belong, to own the latest gadget, to be one of the cool guys.

'So, what's the plan?' said Electra. 'I want to go to the Fur Shop – I've heard they've got the latest calf leggings in stock. And then we could all meet up at the FoodTac booth. What do you think, Josh?'

I could hardly breathe, thrilled both by her suggestions and the fact that she had mentioned me by name.

The Fur Shop was based on the latest craze for clothing made from animal pelts and skins. It started after tons of people stopped eating meat, when they realised that the use of antibiotics on cows and pigs had contaminated the human food chain. It was the antithesis of what my family and my community stood for, and I had never been allowed to go before.

And the FoodTac trend, all the rage for City dwellers, sounded amazing with an emphasis on the tactile sensations of eating food rather than just the taste. I yearned to be part of this fast-moving culture of extremes.

'Sounds fantastic,' I said, immediately wishing I had sounded less enthusiastic as the others looked on with condescension in their eyes.

I RARELY WENT to The Complex, a vast out-of-town shopping mall. It was overwhelming. The non-stop advertising from massive screens gave it a surreal, heady atmosphere, with shoppers inspired by the dream of a better life all trying to surpass their fellow citizens. Electra and her friends had money to burn and competed with one other to buy the most outrageous fur accessory (won by Tom, in my opinion, with a scarf made from inter-twined pigs' tails) and to select the most shocking food (again Tom, for a dish based on the feel and texture of sheep's eye balls).

But I didn't have much money. Dad had given up his well-paid job in the City to move to The Commons and what little savings he'd had were invested in the co-operative. Of course, I understood why. Before he had been a shadow of the man he was now, working long hours, stressed out, not seeing us from dawn to dusk, chasing the illusory golden egg. Now he was a valued leader of the commune, respected both for his knowledge of growing organic vegetables and for his unstinting generosity in helping others. Dad was happy, even I could see that, but that didn't make my situation any easier. Deep down I knew the simple life that my family had chosen was right for them, but I still hankered after being accepted by the City kids.

To try to impress Electra I bought an ice-cream from FoodTac that simulated the consistency of octopus tentacles. Artificial marine-themed dishes were fashiona-ble, ever since the plastic pollution in our oceans had meant that eating fish was deemed a serious health risk. But the pressure to fit in, combined with the heat and the frankly disgusting texture of the ice cream, caused me to throw-up violently. Vomit splattered across the highly polished chrome table. I stared at the mayhem in front of me, mortified, cursing my stupidity and childishness. Running from The Complex, tears in my eyes, the mocking tone of Tom's cries rang in my ears, made worse by the accompanying peals of laughter from Electra and her mates.

I didn't see the car. I was in a rage as I pedalled furiously down the cycle path back to The Commons. I shot onto the highway through the gap in the hedge. The driverless electric vehicle had no chance. Although they had been proven to be safer than human drivers, they still relied on other road users to drive in a predictable manner, and an irate teenager on a bike flying out of a hedge at fifteen miles an hour was not that. The lady in the car glanced up from painting her nails, wondering why her car had come to a sudden stop. I was thrown violently into the air and landed in the ditch on the side of the road, motionless.

I REMEMBER LITTLE about the collision or the aftermath, save for some brief glimpses of blue flashing lights, beeping machinery, sterile operating theatres, and an antiseptic hospital bedroom. I woke up two weeks later in the guest room of the Shared House. It was simply furnished, with a double bed, a plain upright chair next to it, a large wooden wardrobe, two deep armchairs, and a dressing table with a small mirror. A bronze statue of the Buddha stood on one end of the dressing table. An incense stick smouldered on a small stand by its side, scenting the room with lavender. Two beautifully embroidered dream catchers hung by the window. And on the wall by the door, three brightly coloured children's drawings were pinned up, all pictures of a stick human, presumably me, standing in a green field with the sun shining down. *Get Well Soon, Josh* was scrawled across the top of each in alternate red, green and yellow crayon. I smiled, imaging the concentrated efforts of the Toddler Group downstairs.

I wondered why I was in the Shared House, rather than my bedroom back home, a small two-bedroomed eco-build shared with my parents and younger sister. Then I realised it was probably much easier for the community to care for me here. Over the next few days lots of community members took turns to visit me, feed me, bathe me, clothe me. I was rarely on my own for long and even when I dozed I was vaguely aware of the quiet, watchful presence of one of the community nursing me.

The comparison with my grandfather's illness, and subsequent death, five years earlier, was striking. Papa had lived alone in the North, a three-hour train journey away, and had no relatives close by. His life in later years had become increasingly housebound as he became less mobile, so that other than the care nurses, the only people he saw were my family when we visited every first Sunday of the month. I remembered the small, one-bedroom bungalow, tucked at the end of a narrow cul-de-sac, where no traffic ventured. The melancholy atmosphere of neglect and the obvious signs of a life lived in the confines of a shrinking universe. The haunting smell of stale urine mixed with the aroma of past meals on unwashed dishes, evidence of which was often speckled down the front of Papa's thread-worn jumper. The single toothbrush in the tin mug in the bathroom; the well-worn armchair in the corner of the living room, facing the always-on TV; the collection of meals-for-one stacked neatly in the freezer. The sadness in my Papa's eyes as we prepared to return home, that pleading look even as he bravely voiced the mandatory cliché of not wanting to be a burden. How different to the way we look after our older members here.

If I propped myself up against my plump pillows, I could see out of the window onto The Commons grounds below. The Shared House was situated in one corner of the open space that formed the centre of the community. This was taken up with a combination of gardens, wild spaces, a play area, and allotments, with vegetable plots and fruit trees. On both sides were a row of terraced houses, twelve on each side, varying in size, all colourfully decorated in complementary paints. At the far end stood the communal workshops and art room, all with solar panels on the roof that sparkled in the late afternoon sun.

Several benches were scattered around the grounds and I could often spot my friends hanging out together. I watched people tending the allotments, mending buildings, repairing bicycles. Downstairs in the Shared House living room I could hear various activities throughout the day – the Toddler Group, of course, but also a foreign language class, a sewing club, some joint music practice, and the intermittent sound of the table tennis table. And the weekly preparation of the community meal, when everyone would come together to eat and enjoy each other's company.

As my strength gradually returned, the atmosphere in my room became lighter. Not least for my parents, who had been at my bedside every day since the accident, as they visibly relaxed and resumed their carefree natures. Dad became his happy, joking self, banned for a while from making me laugh in case I split the stitches in my back. And Mum feeding me up, with delicious home-made pies and sweets that she knew were my favourites.

Other members of the community came to see me. Old Muriel took it upon herself to visit every afternoon and sit with me quietly for an hour, reading from an anthology of poems dating back to her childhood. Even Parker, one of the founding members, paid occasional visits, keen to discuss the more ethical aspects of my recent adventure. And of course, my mates came around, boisterous, unruly, disrespectful – giving me a hard time for the accident and teasing me mercilessly about the ice-cream incident, which of course had been the talk of the school. Not that Electra, Tom or any of the other City kids had felt the need to get in touch.

I woke from a Saturday afternoon nap to see George

sitting on the chair next to my bed. She was dressed in tight blue jeans, white sneakers, and a royal blue sweatshirt with The Commons yellow crest on it. She had obviously been working at the community's shop, which sold our excess fruit and vegetables, as well as art and craftwork made by the members. As a going concern it was barely profitable, but the idea was to reach out to the local neighbourhood to show them the life that we led.

She had always been just plain George to me, one of the gang, as we grew up together, exploring, experimenting, just mucking around. But now I noticed the golden shine to her auburn hair as it caught the sunlight streaming through the window, the fine freckles across the top of her nose, and the cute dimple in her left cheek as she glanced at me. Gently she reached out and stroked my arm, sending an electric tingling through my body.

'You idiot, you could have killed yourself,' she said, quietly.

'I know.'

Then she paused, sat back, playing with the thin gold chain around her neck. 'Electra Peters, eh?'

'I know.'

We were silent for several minutes. George had her arms crossed now, her eyes staring down at her feet. She shook her head gently. 'You'll never learn, will you?'

I said nothing, just looked back into her eyes, which glistened with tears. Slowly she got up and went out of the room, leaving the door wide open behind her.

The familiar sound of The Eagles' Desperado drifted up from the kitchen below. The musky aroma of her perfume filled the air, as Don Henley's dulcet tones explored the choice between the Queen of Diamonds or the Queen of Hearts.

STILL WATERS

David Butler

AFTER THE ESTATE flooded for the third time, Clodagh swore she'd never return. The thought of the dank interior, silted and filthy, filled her with reptilian loathing. She left Becky with her sister and was seen moving like a sleepwalker along Bridge Street. Before striking out in the direction of the weir, she placed the front-door key in an envelope, with only the address scribbled on it, and pushed it through the bank's quick-deposit shoot.

THE SPEED OF the first flood had been chilling. In the space of a night hour, the water had swollen from runnels, leap-frogging the tarmac to a waist-deep inundation upon which boxes, toys and furniture bobbed and bumped. In the pale halo of a hand torch, a fridge rolled its flippant back. So sudden had the upsurge been, so overwhelming, that neighbours half-dressed waded in and out of unlit houses, laughing, scarcely knowing what to save and what to abandon. She'd shivered on the high ground in pyjamas and dressing-gown, soothing the baby, watching the efforts of Kyle and the others with a detachment that was, almost, amused.

For weeks not a single resident of the estate had been able to return. Long after the waters receded, walls stripped of tide-marked wallpaper exhaled river-breath which blow heaters failed to dry entirely. Once the insurance assessors had ticked their peremptory clip-boards, carpet and underlay, lino and flooring had been pulled up and dumped over the limbs of chairs and prostrate tables in great communal mounds to the head of every terrace. Only the electricals had been taken away for specialist disposal.

At least it had been a shared catastrophe. In the hostels where those without options were variously lodged, a grim camaraderie prevailed. Besides, the inundation had been countrywide; an event which the forecasters declared a once-in-a-century occurrence. If compensation was slow in coming and not remotely commensurate with actual costs, the cheques went some way towards restoring morale. Neighbours began to talk up that night as a disaster movie they'd all survived, a shipwreck in a midlands town. There was much talk of a communal lawsuit which, as months went by, failed to materialise. Late November, on the anniversary, Clodagh's terrace held a party out on the common that was enlivened by fireworks.

In spite of the freak weather event the forecasters had described, the new premiums had either shot up exorbitantly or else contained a clause that excluded compensation in the case of flooding. This was when Clodagh and Kyle had their first real dispute. For an American, Kyle was cautious. Arguably, it was his careful temperament that had landed them on the new estate in the first place. She'd wanted the semi out on the Dublin Road that would, admittedly, have stretched their monthly repayments above the fifteen hundred they'd fixed upon. That said, the sixty thousand down was her money, a legacy from her mother. The property would be in her name. She should have gone with her instinct. But Kyle could do no wrong in those days. Besides, she'd been pregnant, and who knew what unexpected costs a baby might entail.

His caution notwithstanding, it was she who now argued for the extra cover. Kyle, with trademark smirk, attempted to play down the mathematical chances of another inundation with an argument a child could see through. She knew damn well you couldn't '*times it by a hundred, Clo, just do the math. We could buy a couple more houses for that kinda dough.*' At the same time, a fivefold hike in the premium payment was outrageous. It would be difficult to meet, particularly now her maternity leave was unpaid. Becky was autistic, and needed a level of care she was loath to entrust to strangers.

Her stubbornness on the point surprised Kyle. She'd always deferred when it came to matters financial. 'Honey, I know you're upset, but come on…'

'Tell you what we'll do,' she said, brightly. 'We'll ask Dee.'

'Dee? What the hell's Dee got to do with any of this?'

At least Dee works up in the Financial Centre, she thought. She didn't say it. Nor did she bring up the semi on the Dublin Road. She waited until he'd set off for work, then Skyped her sister.

After the call she felt deflated, even humiliated. Dee agreed with a roll of her eyes that of course you couldn't *times it by a hundred, just do the math.'* She'd never thought quite so highly of Kyle Bradley. That said, what it came down to was Becky. To meet the sort of excess Clodagh was talking about, she'd have to go back to teaching fulltime. Bar everything else, that fivefold hike (*fivefold?* Jesus!) was out of their reach any time soon, with so much refurbishment still to be broached. Face it, darling, he's got a point…

'Okay,' she said to Becky, once the computer screen went black. 'But I can't say I'm happy about it.'

FOUR YEARS WENT by before the second flood. In the interim, Clodagh discovered a talent for economising. It became a fixation. It was born of necessity; the school where she'd taught, though most understanding, could no longer hold the position open for her. When Kyle was away, she thought nothing of illegally strapping Becky into the baby seat beside her, collapsing the rear seats and driving ten or even twenty miles to a house clearance or a car boot sale. She became adept at surfing the second-hand websites and second-guessing which were scams. She ended up sourcing bargains for half the terrace.

She put together a glasshouse and tool-shed. And in the face of Kyle's hoisted eyebrow, she developed a real knack for DIY, and even earned the respect of the floor-hands in Woodie's. With business taking Kyle increasingly back to the States, she had something of a free hand about the house.

THERE WAS NO lack of warning this time round. If the first flood had stolen in like a thief in the night, the second arrived with the inevitability of an advancing army. All summer – it was the wettest on record – a swollen sky had loured over the entire country, dumping its excess onto an earth already saturated. For days as she walked with Becky through the fine drizzle along the river, Clodagh had watched with tightening gut the bloated current squirm between the banks like a restive anaconda. Towards the town, teams of men in hardhats, the Fire Brigade, and even a truckload of bawdy soldiers had begun to bolster the flood defences with sack upon sack of wet sand, while a pair of yellow diggers like monstrous toys rattled to dredge the riverbed. High time, because with each bulletin, the contour maps tracked the gradual approach of a double depression across the Atlantic.

On the Thursday she called Kyle. He was in Portland, Oregon, in all likelihood unaware of the impending disaster. As it happened, he wasn't unaware. He'd been keeping abreast of developments on the net. 'Honey, do you know what time it is?'

'Yeah. Listen I need you back here.'

'Huh?'

'It's happening again Kyle. It's going to happen again.' Silence. Static. 'I can't cope alone.'

'What about Dee? Hun, move in with Deirdre till the worst is over. Will you do that for me?'

'Kyle. We need you back here.'

A long silence. 'No can do.' She waited. 'I *told* you this, baby, I explained I…' But what it was he'd told her he didn't get to repeat, or if he did, it was into a dead connection.

She spent Friday emptying cupboards and hauling what could be moved up the stairs to Becky's room, or her own, or the bathroom. She hauled boxes filled with linen and books, CDs and pictures. She hauled up lamps, the TV and the music-system. She rescued the dinner set, the espresso machine, the kettle and microwave. The fridge she emptied into a Tupperware drawer which she laid in the bath, alongside the perishables and foodstuffs. A number of times, she sat inert for so long that Becky tugged at her. It wasn't from exhaustion, precisely. Her eye would fix unseeing on the washing machine or the cooker, on the glasshouse or tool-shed, on the sofa or the fireplace or the parquet floor, her mind vacant. Dee, who'd driven all the way from Dublin straight from work, collected Becky and a bag of her things; Clodagh scarcely roused herself to thank her.

That evening, and through the night, the terrace mounted its own vigilante action. Civil Defence had deposited several van-loads of sandbags and booms which they worked to plug up each gate and doorway to the height of a child. On their macs and umbrellas, the persistence of rain was pure sound. Only within the wasps' nest about each streetlight were the orange darts momentarily galvanised. It was hard to comprehend how they presaged a deluge.

There was markedly less humour this time round. Laughter was nervous and mirthless; cordiality strained by those pulling less than their weight, those occupied with their own properties to the exclusion of all else. The river was due to peak in the early afternoon. If the riverbanks could contain it, or if the overspill was limited, the glutted beast might just pass the estate without soiling it.

By eleven they'd done all that might reasonably be done. Nothing remained but to wait and watch and hope. Maggie Ryan, who was eighty-one, brought out a tray of coffee mugs, and another with sandwiches. They ate them in silence. By noon, the waters began to accumulate about the storm drains and the verges. Slowly, a reflective sheen spread over the roads and the common. Word was that somewhere near the boat club, a wall had subsided. Once the water began to climb their rampart of sandbags, they handed out an arsenal of spades and yard-brushes, of buckets and containers with which to bail. There sounded the indefatigable chug of a water pump on loan from a building site that coughed gouts of yellow seepage back into the flood.

The level continued to inch up. Outside the dyke, a vast drab tide was drifting endlessly south.

Still they hoped.

When the blow fell, it sickened like a betrayal. A literal stab in the back. Maggie Ryan, whose house was on the lowest ground, stumbled from her doorway, deploring what was just then sobbing up over her toilet-bowl. They ran to look, and saw that the floor was awash. One after another, the houses succumbed. Liquid, oily and foul-smelling, surged up through the drains and outlets with a hydraulic logic they could no longer counter. It was neither as deep nor as precarious as the first flood, but even as the bulwark of sandbags held and the main danger passed, the entire terrace was infiltrated with an ankle-deep, rust-coloured slick infected with sewage. Even the men broke down.

IT TOOK SEVERAL months before Clodagh consented to move back. Kyle had installed himself in an upstairs bedroom, throwing himself vociferously into a new lawsuit to nail '*that son-of-a-bitch that built the estate on a goddamn floodplain, for Christ-sakes.*' She knew as well as he that this crusade was to compensate for the fall-off in work, now that his company was downsizing; for his lack of foresight in refusing flood cover; for his unforgiveable absence in the face of the enemy. Having lived there ten weeks, he'd cleared out the ground floor and had it decontaminated, but little else. It remained cold, and musty, and entirely bare.

'Where's Becky?' he'd asked. 'She's not with you?'

'I'm leaving her with Dee,' she said. And that was that. Until such time as the place could be called a home, that's where their child would remain. Looking at their bedroom, strewn with mounds of papers, with a jumble of his laundry behind the door and even several plates and pizza boxes, she added, 'I'm moving into Becky's room.'

Having Kyle about the place made Clodagh realise how much she'd appreciated his absences over the previous few years. At first she felt constrained, as though she were constantly being watched. Soon, though, in their uneasy truce, it was tacitly understood that the restoration of the ground floor was her domain; his business was to shore up the support of the estate in the pursuit of communal legal redress. To be fair to him, he was tireless in this. When, as early as the second evening, she'd mentioned over a glass of wine 'you do know the developer filed for bankruptcy two years ago,' he'd sat back for a minute, shuffled a few thoughts, and declared *'then we'll go after the councillors, and that cowboy architect, and the whatchacallem civil engineers and whatever other sons-of-bitches signed off on this disaster-zone in the first place.'*

She painted. She papered. She scraped. She sought out bargains. But with little of the zeal that had marked her first mission. There was an oppressive weariness about the entire estate that was difficult to escape. A number of *For Sale* signs mouldered over the course of that year. Maggie Ryan's house was boarded up, and word was she'd moved into a retirement home. With Becky in Dublin and Kyle on half-salary, Clodagh began to look for part-time work. It was fortunate that substitute teaching, when she could find it, paid reasonably well. They'd fallen several months into arrears, but no more than anyone else on the estate. She saw Becky every weekend, but rarely during the week. She even consented to Dee enrolling her in a school with special needs, somewhere in Cabra.

One day, looking over her work – the house was passably inhabitable, but to her eye a show house, no more – she tapped at the door of their former bedroom. 'I think we should sell,' she told him.

'Sell? *How?*'

'This is no life, Kyle.' The lack of fight in her own voice surprised her. 'It's not even a home anymore.'

He stood. He removed the glasses he'd begun to wear and paced as far as the window. With his back to her and his hands in his pockets he examined the view, then slowly shook his head.

'So what are you saying? We wait around for the next big rain, is that it?'

He sighed. Again he shook his head. 'There's three, no, four *For Sale* signs on this street alone, or hadn't you noticed?'

'So what do you propose?'

'What I propose…,' he turned. In the look he fired her, something akin to animosity flared. His glasses back on he began to shuffle through a stack of papers. 'Ok, so what? We sell up? That's your big idea?' Unable to locate the bank-statements he required, he slapped the bundle. 'Clodagh.' Deep breath. 'So this place sells for what? Hundred-fifty, hundred-sixty tops. That's saying we can find some chump dumb enough to take it on, which is by no means certain. Know what that means?'

'No, Kyle. What does that mean?'

'That means, my love, we walk outta here not just with Jack shit, not just with no roof over our heads, but with a legacy debt of a hundred, a hundred-ten grand. See what I'm saying? Take ten years just to clear that sort of figure. I mean, do the math. We're stuck with this, baby.'

A shiver racked her. *That's twice already you fucked up,* she thought, *you do the math.* She looked long at the man, unable even to bring him into focus.

As THOUGH IT were the third term in a diminishing geometric progression, the next flood arrived after an interval of two years. Once again, there was plenty of warning from the Met Office. Hard-hatted men in luminous jackets arrived with their trucks and diggers and sandbags. Clodagh didn't wait around to watch. She took the bus to Dublin, turned down the offer of the camp bed in the spare room where Becky had been sleeping, and installed herself on Dee's sofa. Kyle could stay on and play at sandcastles for all that she cared anymore.

Three days later, in the wake of the inevitable news reports, Clodagh removed the house key from the keyring and laid it flat on the breakfast table. 'Borrow an envelope?'

Dee shook her head. 'You're going to go through with it?'

'Yup.'

'But what will you *do*?'

She shrugged, feeling weightless. To have finally lost is a relief when one has been perpetually losing. 'Don't worry. I know we can't stay here,' she supplied, sticking her tongue out at Becky.

'That's not what I'm asking, Clo.' Dee lifted the key as if it was an artefact from an archaeological dig. 'I mean, what about Mam's money?'

'The *deposit*? My dear, that is well and truly lost.'

'So you'll what? File for bankruptcy, is it?' To fracture the surface of Clodagh's flippancy, Dee slapped the key back onto the table. 'Have you any idea what that would *mean*?'

'You're the financial expert.' Briefly, she frowned. 'People make it out.' Then, to Becky, 'We'll be fine, won't we sweetie?'

Dee wasn't one bit convinced by the display. Her sister was being far too facetious. 'Okay. So what about Kyle?'

'He'll be in a hotel somewhere. The place is knee-deep in water.'

'But I mean... *after.*'

'It's my house, Dee. The deeds are in my name.' Becky had come to her, burrowed her forehead into her shoulder. 'Kyle Bradley has no interest in custody, believe me.' She wondered if Becky knew; a wise child. She placed a palm on the soft hair. 'You'll stay up here with

129

Auntie Dee. Won't you Becks?'

At least Dee had no inkling. 'And if he phones?'

Clodagh considered. Already she could hear the weir's incessant churn. The thrill of vertigo, of letting go. 'Tell him…' All the disdain that had accumulated for seven years was concentrated in her features. 'Tell him the goddamn word is *maths.*'

RE CYCLING

Ros Collins

A RECENT RAIN shower lifted the scent of newly mown grass from the verge. Perfect cycling weather, Sal took a deep breath and set off. On cresting the top of the hill, she allowed herself a fist pump before sailing down the other side. The wind tugged at her ponytail and wafted the sweet fragrance of strawberries towards her from the punnets lying in her basket. At the bottom of the hill, she paused and gazed back. The oak tree that crowned the summit had been her target for what, six months? She smiled triumphantly. Pride swelled her chest at how far she'd come in such a short time. The joy of shedding flowing linens for Lycra continued to surprise her.

A damp morning spent at the allotment—picking the last of the soft fruit and hoeing the soil in readiness for an early potato crop—had filled her with satisfaction. Her mouth watered at the thought of mint flavoured New Jerseys, dripping in butter. Well worth a grimy t-shirt with sweat stains circling her armpits. The soil embedded in the ridges on her hands and knees spoke of a job well done. Honest dirt, her father would have said. Pity he wasn't still alive to witness how she'd changed. All those days he'd tried to persuade her to join him on country walks. Too late now – Sal rubbed her eyes, thinking about Dad still hurt.

She glanced at her watch. 'Damn it.' There'd be no chance of a shower, now. A whizz with the flannel would have to suffice. Impossible to keep track of time at the allotment. She pushed ahead harder, faster, her heart beating to the rhythm of the pedals. On reaching the small cottage she and Dan called home, Sal slammed her bike against the low brick wall and jogged down the path. Once inside, she bounded up the stairs, pulling her top over her head as she headed for the bathroom. Five minutes later, with her favourite peasant skirt covering the brown smudges she'd failed to wash off, Sal was ready.

She grabbed a rucksack, already filled with notes and photographs, and raced back to her bike. Today already threatened to be a challenge so being late would only make it worse. The prospect of an audience filled with bored teenagers had been giving her sleepless nights. Upright on the pedals, she wove through the busy streets towards St David's Girls' School.

Passionate about her new self-image, Sal wanted to spread the word, inspire the next generation to commune with nature, share her enjoyment of cycling in the fresh air. What better way than to visit schools in the area? So far she'd enjoyed classes of spellbound seven and eight-year-olds but this was altogether different. Last night Dan had lost his cool with her, unable to understand her nervous tossing and turning.

'Just be yourself,' he'd said. 'They'll love you. Now for goodness sake, get some sleep.'

Sal swept onto the school grounds, hair sticking to her sweaty forehead. The solitary bike rack only accommodated six cycles. Jeez, what century was this school living in? Fingers fumbling, she jammed a chain through her crossbar and looped it around a drainpipe, snicking the padlock closed.

Pleased the strawberries had survived the journey; she popped one into her mouth—a fruity alternative to Dutch courage—and strode across the playground with the punnets. The secretary, a small round woman, struggled to her feet as Sal clattered into reception, her rucksack snagging the door handle.

'Good afternoon, Mrs Elliott.' She offered her hand. 'The head has put you in the hall—too many girls signed up to fit into a classroom.'

Sal's heart plummeted; she much preferred a cosy environment.

'Oh, please call me Sally. I expect the girls imagined I'd be more interesting than a maths lesson.' She forced a laugh. 'Would you like a strawberry? I picked them this morning.'

'Mmm, they're so sweet.' After licking her fingers the secretary put the punnets on a desk overflowing with paper.

Lips pursed, Sal stroked the logo on her cotton top: *Save paper, save trees.*

Oblivious, the administrator barrelled ahead, calling over her shoulder, 'Come this way, and I'll take you to the assembly hall.'

As they neared the dark-wood double doors at the end of the corridor the hub-bub of chatter grew louder.

'In you go dear, they don't bite.' Patting Sal on the arm, her guide waddled back to the office.

Left alone, it took all of Sal's steel to open the door and walk up the aisle. The thrum of voices stilled as dozens of eyes peered from beneath long fringes to watch her progress. The Head, a well-dressed woman in her forties, stood next to the stage, nose buried in a document and Sal coughed to announce her arrival.

'Ah, Mrs Elliott, you're here, good, good.' She looked at her watch, 'I'm afraid you'll only have twenty minutes before the girls' next lesson.'

Sally found herself propelled back to her own school days. The miniscule tightening of the principal's lips, followed by the metaphorical slap on the wrist for tardiness, knocked off fourteen years. And why hadn't she taken more care with her appearance? She pulled a tissue from her sleeve and dabbed her hot forehead.

'Sorry I'm on the drag, I had difficulty finding somewhere to leave my bike.' Nothing to be lost by having a quick dig, though Sally lightened her words with a smile.

'I'll introduce you, and then I'm afraid I must be off. But my deputy's sitting at the back if you need anything.'

Thirty seconds later Sal was centre stage. Where were the rapt, upturned faces of her primary school audiences? Instead, a sea of heads bowed, fingers picked at peeling nail polish or rubbed at knobby polyester skirts. She tossed her notes back into the rucksack and studied the girls. Dry statistics tracking climate change simply wouldn't hack it.

Her brain had the consistency of thick porridge and the task of getting her thoughts in order made her armpits prickle. Where to begin? She cleared her throat.

'Just over a year ago I was fat, very fat.' There wasn't a sound in the hall. 'A lifestyle consisting of eating chocolate biscuits, drinking cans of cola, and lounging on the settee with my laptop settled rolls of blubber around my midriff.'

One or two girls gazed up, raking over Sal's figure with critical aplomb.

'I was born a hopeless timekeeper, and one morning last year, I'd left it late to go to a dental appointment.' She smiled. 'No matter, our shiny Range Rover sat in the garage and I'd be there in no time.'

A few more heads lifted.

'Only it didn't.'

A mock gasp rippled along the rows. Drama queens, every one of them.

'Where'd it gone, Miss?' someone called.

'I hadn't the foggiest.' Sal shrugged. 'Maybe my husband had taken it for a service on his way to work and forgotten to tell me. In my head I went through every possible scenario until—' She paused, trying to squeeze a morsel of tension into her voice. 'I saw, tucked in the corner of the garage, a bicycle with an enormous pink bow attached to the handlebars.'

Giggles ricocheted around the hall but at least there was a smattering of interest.

'It dawned on me.' Sal tapped the side of her forehead with a finger. 'Something we'd discussed after a glass of wine had actually happened. Our lovely car had been sold and replaced by two cycles.' Now she had the attention of all but the back rows; the older girls. 'My husband works at Minsmere Nature Reserve and always wanted to do more for the environment.'

'My mum would have had a hissy fit,' said a pretty girl sitting in the second row. 'She'd have thrown my dad out.'

More snickers erupted.

'Yeah, I reckon your husband is a real plonker.' At this, the deputy leapt to his feet in an attempt to identify the speaker, his eyebrows knitted.

'Well, I was pissed off too, I can tell you.' Sal ignored the mental darts aimed at her from the teacher. 'Frosty the Snowman joined us for supper that evening, but it turned out to be the best thing that could have happened.' She slapped her hand on the podium. 'Overnight my life changed. I had to plan my days more carefully, shop locally, and get to grips with an overgrown allotment. But best of all enjoy the countryside. We're lucky to live in such a beautiful part of the country.'

The older madams still fidgeted, Sal needed to bring them closer.

'Gradually, by cycling every day, I became fitter and all the excess weight slipped away.'

Time to prove the point; Sal wasn't afraid of a dash of drama herself. She unzipped her skirt and stepped out of it to reveal the tight black shorts she'd kept on. Confident her athletic figure would impress, she gave a little twirl. Aha, now she had them.

'See, it's a win-win situation. By doing my bit for the planet I get to have a figure pretty similar to Jessica Ennis.'

'Who's she?' a lone voice called and Sal laughed.

Of course, Jessica had been *her* role model; these girls probably hadn't a clue about the diminutive athlete with a washboard stomach.

'Ariana Grande. Wouldn't mind her bod. She's well

fit,' called another. Murmurs of agreement followed.

'Sorry, I'm showing my age, but seriously, you should try it. The summer's coming and it's wonderful to be outside. The more people riding bikes, the healthier we'll all be.' Sal turned to a blank page on the adjacent flip chart. 'Okay girls, get your thinking caps on, and give me some ideas of how you can do your bit for the planet.'

The felt-pen squeaked as Sal hurried to transcribe their propositions: banning plastic, money-back schemes for bottles, using public transport instead of taking the car, stop eating beef, more water fountains in public buildings. For a while their suggestions came like shotgun fire.

As their ideas tailed off, an older girl stood in the aisle to make her point.

'We've only got one bike stand, Mrs Elliott. It's pathetic. There's nowhere for us to leave our bikes, so we don't bring them.'

Her earnest expression gave Sal an idea.

'Hmm, I noticed that when I arrived and it got me thinking. How about organising a fund raiser to source more racks? I'd be happy to help you, sorry, what's your name?'

'Cassie.'

'Okay, Cassie, I'll talk to the Head on the way out and see if we can sort something.'

Warmth coursed through her with the realisation that here was a generation who genuinely cared about their environment. It didn't have to be the doom and gloom picture the news media described.

A bell pealed in the corridor and the deputy strode to the stage. 'Girls, I'm sure you'll want to join me in thanking Mrs Elliott for coming in today and giving us a most entertaining and thought-provoking talk.'

Heat bloomed in her cheeks at the sound of the applause. 'It has been my pleasure.' She gave a little bow, before turning to gather her belongings. No point in putting her skirt back on for the ride home, so she stuffed it into her rucksack. From nowhere, cold fingers curled over her arm and her head snapped around.

'Goodness, you made me jump.'

A short girl with pigtails stared up at her. 'I'm going to ask my mum to sell her car. We don't need it.' The girl sucked on the loose hair at the bottom of one of her braids. 'Smoke pours out of the exhaust and pollutes the street. There are toddlers on our road. It's bad for them to breathe in all those fumes.' Then, like the sun peeping from behind a cloud, a smirk washed the gravity from her face. 'You've still got mud on your knees, Miss.'

Before Sal could reply, she'd scampered off in the direction of her two friends. Arms around each other, the trio jostled and laughed their way to the next lesson.

All thoughts of the planet abandoned, she stared at her knees—the knees she'd exposed on stage—crusted with dried garden muck.

APIS MELLIFERA

Jane Crowley

I WOKE TO a dull droning sound at the window of my bedroom. As I lay in bed listening, trying to place it, the noise was punctuated with a regular flat chiming – like the sound when you flick a china vase with a crack running through it.

I got up and went to the window to find a honey bee lying exhausted on the sill. It must have been flying into my window pane for the past few minutes and concussed itself. It was bigger than I had remembered honey bees being, and I could clearly see the fine golden hairs lining its abdomen and thorax, the shiny jet of its articulated legs. I opened the window to allow it to fly away, but it sat there, cleaning its antennae listlessly.

When I came back to my bedroom later in the day it was motionless in the same place: dead.

The death of the honey bee left me with an unsettled, depressed feeling, even though the day was bright and clear and I had no good reason to be upset. I tried to put the thought out of my mind.

I WAS DIGGING in a new pear tree when Ana came lurching towards me through clouds of fennel fronds. She looked like an astronaut crashing back to Earth in her beekeeper's suit, trailing smoke from one gloved hand. There was a soft thump as she landed on her backside next to me, crushing my newly planted line of runner beans.

She removed her hat and threw it behind her, mauling the few seedlings not already damaged by her heavy descent. I have always struggled not to stare at Ana. She's hard to look away from, and if you catch her smile it is impossible not to smile along with her. On this particular afternoon she looked a little strained around the eyes, a little despondent.

'They're restless today. I think I've lost my queen.'

'Oh, I'm sorry. How can you tell?'

'Instinct.' She laughed 'No, not really. When they sense the queen is failing, they start building these little hanging cells on the bottom of the comb. It's no problem. They'll quickly make a new one to take her place.'

'*Make* a new one? That sounds so Frankenstein-y. I always thought they, I don't know, *elected* one or something.'

I thought she might die laughing at that point. In any

case, there were tears in her eyes when she finally stopped convulsing. I decided not to confess that I had been entirely serious, and that I still didn't know the first thing about bees, despite occupying the allotment next to East Croydon's premier beekeeper for the best part of three years: a fault made particularly egregious by the fact that it was almost certainly due to her bees that my plants continued to produce enough fruit and vegetables to keep me fed all year round.

'Now you've composed yourself, would you kindly remove yourself from my runner bean patch? Your arse is quite sizable enough to damage my poor little green friends.'

She stretched her arms behind her head and shuffled a few inches to the left. It would have to do.

I was perhaps overly protective of my allotment crops, each one being a hard-fought triumph over my north-facing flat and tiny windowsills, and my own inability to remember to water anything. One day I planned to get a greenhouse and lavish my little seeds and striplings with all the attention they deserved, but giving up precious planting space was a difficult choice to make.

Ana had no such problems. I had been there the day that she planted up her plot, all the new-tilled earth damp and grey-brown, exposed to the air. When people talk about earth they use such rich colours: deep chocolate-brown, parched red, loamy humus-rich black; but, from my experience, it's all greyish once you get right down to it, or at least, it is when you're talking about inner city gardening.

Still, even grey city dirt is capable of supporting all kinds of luxuriant plant life, and so Ana's preferred method of haphazardly scattering armfuls of seed – fennel, phlox, sweet peas and stocks, even lavender (which I had never dared grow from seed as it is notoriously pernickety) – seemed to work just fine. The rose bushes she had dug in at seemingly random spots had never once been pruned or treated, to my knowledge.

The result was a sprawling jungle of leggy plants with no order or reason and, because it was Ana's, it was perfect.

'I won't grow anything that doesn't smell glorious,' she told me. 'If it smells good, then it will make tasty honey. The rest of it doesn't matter. I want my honey to be the sweetest and most floral it can be. Of course, having your turnip farm next door isn't helping. If my honey tastes cruciferous this year, I'm blaming you.'

That was always the point of her allotment: to be a standing buffet for her bees. It seemed to work, particularly in the late afternoon and early evening, when the scent of all the collected plants would rise in a fragrant mist, and hundreds upon hundreds of little carapaced bodies would buzz lazily around each flower head, greedily drinking in the nectar.

But now her queen was dead, or dying.

'I mean, you almost never see the queen,' she said. 'It's not like I got to know her in any particular way, but somehow I was always quite attached to her. Just knowing she was in there keeping the hive in order, making sure everything was working as it should, was comforting.

Bees are amazing, really. They're not really lots of individual creatures; each hive is almost like a superorganism, with each individual bee being one body part, if you see what I mean. The hive doesn't suffer from losing the queen. I don't know why I'm upset about it really.'

I wanted most to hold her hand, but with those ridiculous oven-mitts that she used to protect them from rogue stings it seemed a pointless gesture.

'I suppose she was the only organised bit of your whole allotment,' I joked. 'With everything else so messy she was the little ruler that kept everything in line.'

'I suppose she was.'

We sat in silence for a while, eyes fixed in the middle distance, looking at nothing in particular, breathing in the smell of crushed greens. When she spoke again I jumped, having almost forgotten she was there, if such a thing were possible.

'I've never been a very tidy person. Anything I start always ends in a pickle one way or another: jobs, family, friends. I just don't keep track of things. I forget and I don't plan and I manage to alienate everyone. Keeping bees is the only thing I've ever managed to do that needed any kind of routine. It's tiring, honestly, falling and flailing your way through life like I do. I always wanted to be a woman like you: practical, sorted, always going in the right direction.'

'Good grief is that what you think of me? I've no idea about anything! I panic and worry and try to draw neat little lines around things to make everything knowable and understandable, and it still doesn't work. I've always admired the chaos, the spontaneity, the sort of joyful creative madness that you have. You're just *you*, and that's just about the highest compliment I can pay you.'

She looked right at me then, and there was a small smile playing around the corners of her eyes where fine wrinkles bunched and gathered.

'You admire me then?'

Did I imagine the archness? The smile was still there. Something washed over me from the prickling soles of my feet to the tops of my ears, which I already knew had flushed red.

'I – always.'

Suddenly we were both laughing hysterically, uproari-ously, painfully.

The bees, startled, rose up in a swarm and we were surrounded by a deep rhythmic buzzing sound as the two of us clutched each other in the warm, sweet air of our own little Eden.

ATTRACTING SONGBIRDS
Kimberly Christensen

ONE DAY I woke up and started thinking about how I hadn't heard a single bird sing in God-knew-how-many years. I live on the twentieth floor of my building so there's plenty of shrieking from gulls, cooing pigeons and squawking crows, but no actual birdsong.

'Computer, how do you attract songbirds?' I asked.

'Songbirds need food, water, shelter and nesting sites,' it answered.

A bird feeder, perfect.

'Computer, order a bird feeder,' I instructed. 'And a bag of birdseed.'

Two days later, my phone alerted me that a package was waiting at our building's receiving centre. I stopped in on my way home. I hung the feeder on the balcony and sat by the window for an hour waiting for songbirds to appear. Nothing. The next day I saw a single sparrow. The day following, the seed was gone. A chubby-cheeked squirrel grinned at me from the top of the railing. Urban squirrels are such assholes.

I contemplated a bird bath, wondering if management would let me put it on the rooftop among the solar panels. Probably not.

'Computer, order a birdhouse. And more birdseed. And a squirrel-proof bird feeder.'

Across the alley, the kid who lived in the flat opposite mine watched as I suction-cupped my new birdhouse to the window overlooking my balcony.

'No birds gonna come here,' Junior called to me. 'Ain't enough trees.'

'You know why there aren't enough trees?' I called back. 'The adults don't like them because they're messy and they can't get any of you to rake leaves. You're too attached to your video games.'

Junior puffed out his chest. 'That ain't true. I do chores.'

To be fair, I'd seen him hauling his family's recycling to the chute and wheeling his rolling cart home from the grocery store. Junior was all right, for a kid.

'Would you take care of a tree?' I asked him.

'Sure would.'

'You got yourself a deal.'

The computer wouldn't order me a tree though it did suggest a crab apple to attract robins, bluebirds and waxwings. I dragged my rolling cart on two subways and a bus, out to the suburbs to pick up the tree. It turned out to only be about three feet tall, with a skinny little trunk not even as wide as a baseball bat. That tree was only going to produce three crab apples, at most. Oh well, it was a start.

Junior and I had to take turns with the pickaxe I borrowed from the maintenance gal to make a hole deep enough for a tree in the strip in front of our building. There was a dirt circle already there, which at one point they probably meant to fill with a tree. We didn't ask permission. I figured it would be a while before they noticed.

I found Junior watering the tree after school the next day with water he had caught in his shower. Neither of us knew how much water it needed, but we figured it was probably better to overwater than under.

'Maybe you could do a little research,' I suggested to Junior. 'On the internet.'

His face brightened. The kid liked plants, apparently. Or feeling useful. Or maybe both.

Turned out, I shouldn't have got him so excited about the tree because a couple of nights later, somebody came by and broke it. I woke up in the morning to see a snapped trunk sticking up out of the hole that Junior and I had laboured over. The poor tree hadn't even had time to attract a single damn bird.

I figured it would be better for Junior to hear it from me, so I put on some clothes and went across the skybridge to the building next door. Junior opened the door still in his pyjamas.

'I'm afraid I have bad news, Junior. Someone broke our tree.'

Junior walked out to the balcony and leaned over the edge until he could see the sad little stump. The colour drained from his cheeks and his lips pressed together angrily.

'Who would do that?' he demanded.

I shook my head. 'Miscreants.'

'Miss Who?' Junior asked.

'No goods, punks, trouble-makers.'

Junior nodded but I could tell his mind was spinning. 'They wouldn't have done it if they had been the ones watering it,' he said.

I thought that was probably true, but I had no plans to start an afterschool club. Instead I had the computer download some bird calls when I got back home. It felt better than getting my hopes up over a crab apple tree.

I DIDN'T SEE Junior for several months except for a friendly hand wave here and there. Then one day he showed up at my door with a tear-stained face.

'Boots died,' he pronounced.

'Was he the tabby?'

Junior nodded.

'I'm so sorry. He was a nice cat.' I'd liked watching Boots sun himself on Junior's balcony.

'I was wondering…' His voice broke and he struggled not to cry. 'I want to bury him under a tree. I thought maybe you would help?'

'Of course.'

I wanted to remind Junior how upset he'd been when the tree without a cat planted under it had been broken, but I couldn't see the purpose in that. Can't spare people from broken hearts.

'Will your mom let you go to the nursery with me?'

'I'll ask.'

Junior reappeared at my front door a few minutes later with a paper bag, which he handed to me.

'There's $41.57 in there. Do you think that will be enough?'

'I think so. And if not, I'll contribute a bit to Boots' memory as well.'

Junior's face lit up. 'Really? That would be super nice of you.'

'No problem.'

JAMMED SHOULDER-TO-SHOULDER ON the subway, I asked Junior a few of those annoying questions that adults always ask kids: his grade – 6th – and his favourite subject – History – and what he had planned for the summer – Nothing. Then I thought to ask him about Boots and that opened the floodgates.

'This one time, when Boots was little, he got stuck in the Rodriguezes' storage room. He was missing for three days. I finally heard him meowing his head off. I knocked on the door but Carlos' grandma doesn't speak much English so I was telling her 'cat-o' and going 'meow' but she thought I was just losing my mind. I didn't give up though, and she finally followed me downstairs and heard Boots for herself. After that, whenever she saw me, she would say 'cat-o bien?' and would grin real big at me. She brought him milk sometimes too.'

'He was pretty mellow,' I commented. 'Didn't bother the pigeons.'

'Yeah. He was so patient. He let Gracie put paper bonnets on his head and everything.' 'Will Gracie want to help us plant the tree?'

'I think so. Or at least she'll want to throw some dirt on him and say a few words. She's already practicing that part.'

'Will he be buried in a paper bonnet?'

Junior laughed just a little at this. 'I hope not. But I don't think Boots would mind, really.'

'The paper will compost anyway.'

'What's that?'

'Decompose. Break down and help create more soil.'

Junior was silent for a minute. 'Will Boots do that

too…compost?'

'Yep, and the nutrients in Boots will help feed the tree and make it grow strong.'

'So Boots will be in the tree, and when we eat the fruit, we'll be eating Boots? That's weird.'

Now it was my turn to laugh. 'Well, it's kind of like that. And kind of not. But if you think about it that way, then dinosaurs and woolly mammoths and all kinds of creatures are in the food you're eating too. Not to mention the animals you actually set out to eat.'

Junior thought about this. 'Let's get a tree that makes fruit for birds, not people. I don't think I want to eat Boots.'

'No problem. We can get another crab apple or a mulberry.'

'I thought mulberry was a bush.'

'Might be. It's also a tree.'

'Let's get that. Gracie's always singing that rhyme.'

JUNIOR AND I walked up to the first person in a green vest that we saw at the nursery.

'Excuse me. We're looking for a mulberry tree. Do you have any?'

The nursery employee – Marina – was a bit older than me, silver streaks weaving into her black hair. Her face was wrinkled from sun and from smiling. She cracked a smile at us now.

'You guys planting a mulberry tree? Birds love them, you know. A word of advice – don't plant them where you park your car.'

'We live in one of the new urban villages,' I said.

'No car needed,' added Junior, quoting right from the marketing material posted all over our buildings.

'That works. Let's go find you a tree.'

Junior and I eyed half a dozen trees, comparing their heights, the green of their leaves, and the size of their pots. The biggest ones were too far out of our price range.

'That's okay, though,' Junior said comfortingly. 'Remember how hard it was to dig that hole? We don't want to have to make it bigger.'

'Junior, you are wise beyond your years.'

'You have a hole already?' asked Marina. 'About how big?'

Junior and I made circles with our hands and arms. Surprisingly, they were about the same size.

'OK, well you will want enough room for lots of compost and loose soil, so I think you should get one of the smaller trees.'

'We need room for a cat too,' I said.

Marina cast me a questioning glance. I drew my finger across my throat.

'Oh,' she said sympathetically. 'It's a memorial tree. I'm so sorry. What was the cat's name?'

'Boots,' said Junior. 'I want him to have a good tree. The little ones look like twigs.'

'Mulberries grow pretty fast. And they're hardy, so Boot's tree will be difficult to kill. But they also spread pretty easily if there's another one around to fertilize it…'

I shook my head. 'I doubt that will be a problem. Not many trees anywhere in our neighbourhood.'

Marina pulled a four-foot-tall tree to the front. It looked to me like the sort of thing Charlie Brown might plant if his cat died. Marina encouraged Junior to kneel with her by the tree. She showed him the root ball and told him how deep to plant it.

'You'll need to water it a lot to get it started, especially through its first summer. You got a hose?'

'I'm going to catch the water in my house,' Junior said. 'With a bucket.'

Marina looked at me with a raised eyebrow.

'Thirty floor high rise,' I explained. 'If Junior hauls buckets from his house and I haul them from mine, I'm sure we'll manage.'

'Okay. Well, you don't want soapy water, but if you catch it while you're waiting for the water to get warm or if you can set up a rain collection system somewhere that should do pretty well.'

'Got that?' I asked Junior.

He nodded. 'Sounds like something else for me to research.'

'You'll be a tree-watering expert by the time we're done.'

He smiled. I think he stood a little taller too.

Marina loaded the tree onto a cart and helped us to the cash register. I gave Junior his paper bag of money.

'You want some compost too?' Marina asked. 'I think one bag would probably do.'

'Sure,' I said. Might as well give this little tree a fighting chance. Plus, it would give our fellow subway riders something to talk about.

Marina rang the total and waited while Junior counted out his money. He was four dollars short.

Just as I was about to reach into my purse, Marina said, 'Oh wait. I forgot to give you the memorial tree discount.' She re-rang the total. Now Junior had a couple of dollars left over, plus a bag of compost.

Junior lifted the compost into my rolling cart. 'I'll carry the tree,' he said.

Junior beamed the whole way home. We deposited the tree and the compost in the alley. Then Junior went home to get Gracie. He returned a few minutes later without her.

'Mom says we have to have lunch first.'

'That sounds like a good idea.'

I sat on the front step as I ate, keeping one eye on the tree. A group of older kids played basketball farther down the alley. I wondered if any of them had broken the other tree, and how long it would take them to break this one. Maybe I could put a barrier around it. I wished I had thought of that at the nursery. I was contemplating electric cattle fencing when Junior and Gracie arrived, pet carrier in tow.

'Why don't we put Boots in the shade?' I suggested. 'So he stays cool while we get the hole ready.'

Junior found Boots a sheltered spot that we could see from the street. I joined the kids at the sidewalk. Junior did most of the shovelling while Gracie wandered up and down the block scouring the sidewalk cracks for dandelions. She returned with a small bouquet and another girl around her age, which I guessed was about seven.

'This is Cristina,' she said. 'Tina, this is Ms. Turner.'

'Hi Cristina. Are you here to help with Boots' funeral?'

Tina nodded.

'Okay. Well I think we are just about ready.'

Cristina whispered something to Gracie, who then said, 'Don't start without us. We'll be right back.'

Gracie set down her dandelion collection on the sidewalk and ran off with Cristina. Junior was almost done emptying out the hole. I decided to run inside and make sure that I had all the facts about planting a tree straight. I thought maybe the last time I hadn't got it quite right.

'Computer, how do you plant a tree?'

The computer summarised all the steps, which sounded just about like what I had done the last time, except it recommended filling the hole with some water first. That sounded practical, especially since we hadn't had a good rain lately. I grabbed a bucket which I filled from my shower and hauled it back out with me.

A group of kids stood at the sidewalk now, talking to Junior and the girls. I recognised a couple of them as the basketball players, but I swore a couple of them had never stepped foot in our neighbourhood before. Probably spent all their time plugged into their video games.

Junior stood in front of the hole, leaning on the shovel like a veteran farmer. It made me smile. I handed him my bucket.

'The computer recommended putting some water in the hole first and letting it sink in.'

'Could I do that?' a boy asked. He may, or may not, have been Carlos Rodriguez.

'Sure,' Junior said.

The boy poured the water carefully into the hole, where it just sat without sinking in. That ground was bone dry.

'Maybe we could mix some compost in with the water,' I suggested.

The group of kids went to the alley. Two of them hoisted the bag of compost between them. Junior lifted the tree. Gracie carried the pet carrier. Back at the sidewalk, Junior tried to tear open the compost bag with his fingers, but the bag just stretched around them.

'You gotta stab it with the shovel,' said Gracie in a stage whisper.

'How do you know that?' Junior asked.

'I Googled "how to plant a tree" while you and Ms. Turner were at the nursery.'

The bigger kids all laughed but Gracie stood her ground. Junior speared the bag with the blade of the shovel. All the kids dug into the black compost and threw their handfuls into the hole. About half the bag was empty by the time the water was soaked up. Time for the cat.

Junior removed the lid from the pet carrier and lifted out poor stiff Boots. Boots was curled up, but not compactly enough to fit neatly into our hole. One of the girls used the edge of her hand like a bulldozer to scrape back some compost for Boots' belly and feet. Junior tried him at different angles until he finally found a good fit for the damp, muddy cat. Junior rocked Boots back and forth one last time to make sure he was secure. That cat wasn't going anywhere.

Gracie took up her position at the edge of the hole. 'It is with great sadness that we are gathered together today to remember Boots.'

The girl had done her homework, that's for sure.

'Boots was known to all this neighbourhood, and will be missed,' she said in her high, clear voice. She looked at each one of us. 'Would anyone like to offer any words about Boots?'

The kid that I thought might be Carlos cleared his throat. 'My abuelita really liked Boots. He would even let her rub his panza. He gave me a lot of scratches the time I tried it.' The boy showed us the scars on his arm.

'Boots' tongue felt like sandpaper,' said Cristina. 'I liked it when he licked my cheek.'

'Boots liked to ride the elevator sometimes,' said one of the older girls. 'I think he thought he was a person.'

Junior had been holding himself together really well while everyone else spoke. Then there was a silence. I could see him figuring out what he wanted to say.

'Boots was the best pal I could have had. He always knew when I was having a bad day. On bad days, he would cuddle with me until I fell asleep. I'm going to miss that.'

Junior's cheeks flushed, and I knew he was fighting back tears. Poor kid.

I stooped to pick up a handful of compost. 'Goodbye, Boots,' I said. 'The neighbourhood won't be the same without you.'

Gracie followed my lead. 'Bye Boots.'

One by one the other kids tossed in more compost until Boots had a nice blanket of earth covering him. Junior busied himself shaking the tree out of its pot. Every now and then, he wiped a cheek on his shirt, but the other kids gave him space. He broke apart the root ball like Marina had told him. I held the tree over the hole so that he and Gracie could spread its roots out over the cat. Then Junior picked up the shovel and covered the cat and the roots with dirt.

When he was finished, he tapped the loose earth with the back of the shovel. I let go of the tree. It stood pretty straight in its hole.

'Let's water some more,' I suggested.

Gracie poured out the other half of the bucket from my house while Junior ran upstairs to fill another one.

'We need a hose,' one of the kids commented.

'You can catch the water in your shower,' I said. 'That's what Junior and I are going to do – catch the water while we're waiting for it to warm up.'

The kids nodded. Soon enough Junior was back, pouring his bucket onto the tree's base. A depression formed where the water saturated the dirt, but Carlos filled that right up with more of the loose earth. Gracie and Cristina spread their dandelions around the base of the little tree. Then we all stood back to admire it.

'Guess that's it,' said Junior. 'Thanks for coming, everyone.'

The kids all nodded at each other and drifted off. I carried the tools back to the maintenance room. I peeked around the room for fencing but saw none. I made a mental note to pick some up soon.

I HAVEN'T DONE it though. Don't think I need to. One kid or the other stops by that tree twice a day, bringing half a bucket of water or laying dandelions at the tree's base. Gracie and Cristina made little cardboard signs that they hung on each of the tree's five little branches.

RIP Boots.
Gone but not forgotten.
Here lies Boots, best cat in the hood.
Gone to the big litterbox in the sky.
Miss you, Boots.

The tree won't be big enough to produce much fruit for a while and I still haven't seen a single songbird alight in its branches, but now from my window I sometimes hear the voices of the kids singing *All Around the Mulberry Bush*. It beats the sounds of gulls and crows any day.

THE MEETING
David Fell

[Linda]

As soon as I saw him I knew something was odd. He was one of those, not just an outsider – we have plenty of those, obviously – but wrong, you know, dressed in a suit, haircut like he had it trimmed every week, briefcase. A briefcase! I ask you.

Anyway, I was working in the café – the blue one, just off Tulip. I love the café shift, it's my favourite, I think. I just love talking to people and finding out what's going on and getting the feel of how the day is. Not that I mind the other shifts, obviously – it wouldn't work if people minded, I get that – but, well, we all have favourites, don't we? I know Maureen really likes it in the kitchens; she just loves getting all the food ready and thinking about all those people who are going to be well fed. I think she worked in a school kitchen once, but this is much better, she says. All the ingredients are fresh, and she gets to actually make stuff rather than heat up the packets, you know. Maureen's really sweet. She got here only a little while after me so I guess we were both a bit scared together and learned how it all works at the same time. She came here with her husband; he's got early onset dementia, you know, and coming here changed her life, it really did.

Well, it changes all our lives, doesn't it?

Anyway, I was working in the café just off Tulip, like I said, and it was a completely normal morning, to be honest, medium busy, a few mums and a few students and a few people on their laptops, and then this man in the suit walks in and looks the place over and takes a seat by the window over where we keep the big pot plant. It wasn't like in the movies, you know those westerns or gangster films where everyone goes quiet, but it was a bit strange. Just for a moment, a few people looked up and didn't look back down again: this man in a suit, what was he doing here? You could see the same thought happening on a dozen faces at the same time, and then he headed towards the big pot plant and everyone sort of got back to whatever they were doing, you know, doing their schoolwork or playing on their computer or whatever.

I couldn't ignore him, of course, I had to serve him.

I gave him a few minutes. He'd looked at the menu almost as soon as he sat down, but he put it down again just as quickly, so I knew he needed another look. He had these shoes on, not so surprising given the suit and the briefcase and the haircut, but his shoes! It wasn't just that they were new and shiny. It was like, well, you could just see from a glance that they'd cost an arm and a leg, the kind of shoes that come from one of those top-end shops in the old city, one of those places where people with too much money go to buy stuff to try to intimidate the rest of us, you know.

Actually, that's one of the best things about this place. I hadn't really thought about it before I got here. Well, not like that I hadn't. I suppose – before I got here – I'd have been a bit intimidated by those kinds of shoes, and by the kind of man that wears a pair of shoes like that. But at the same time a bit of me secretly admired him, or wanted to know him, or wanted my son James to grow up to be like him. Weird, when you think about. I suppose we all did it, didn't we? Complain about wealthy people but secretly hope we could be one.

But here at Visco it's not like that. Not at all. It takes some getting used to – Maureen still has pangs, I think, even after two years – but after a while you just start to think, what was that all about? Why did I spend so much time worrying about all that? All that time, working hard, desperately trying to get a nicer sofa or a better car or whatever. I remember one year – I feel so ashamed thinking about it now – one year I managed to take me and the children on holiday to Crete and I just went on and on about it to my friends, on and on. And some of it might have been because I was just plain excited but, to be honest, looking back on it now, I was mainly telling everyone I was going to Crete because I knew that it was a better place, a more expensive place, than wherever they were going on holiday that year.

Awful.

And after a few months in Visco what starts to happen – no one tells you this – what starts to happen is you start to feel sorry for them. You know, sorry for everyone who isn't here. Sorry for everyone who's still running around buying things they don't really need just so that they can impress their friends. Sorry for everyone that thinks they need to own a Ferrari. That's pretty much how I felt about this man in the suit. There he was, all uptight and thinking his shoes mattered, but I could see his knee going up and down like the clappers underneath the table and he was clearly so uncomfortable and was probably wondering what on earth he was doing here and I just felt sorry for him.

[Justin]

I TELL YOU, I was so uncomfortable. It had taken me about three hours to get there and the whole place was just bloody strange. Nothing can prepare you, trust me. You can read all the stuff on the website, all the articles, all the briefing papers, all of it. And then suddenly you're standing on the bridge and you see the south-western edge of the city ahead of you and it just looks…different. No tall buildings. No billboards. No cars.

And it's really quiet. You can hear the water and the wind and the birds. Completely different from the old city.

They put you on a bus once you've crossed the bridge. Electric. More like a tram, actually. Not like any tram or bus you've seen, mind. There are loads of them, criss-crossing the city, all decorated differently, some with funky paint jobs, some covered in… well, stuff. I saw one while I was in the café that looked like it was made from seashells. Mad. I mean, why did they do that?

I'd arrived early, even though it had taken me bloody ages to get there. That's one of the things the briefing papers got right, I suppose. And the directions are good, once you get onto the island, not just the physical signposts, the tech, too. The whole place is fully wired, high-speed. I had a good signal everywhere, all the time, so I had no trouble finding the café and I just grabbed a table by the window. The waitress gave me a couple of minutes and I ordered a cappuccino and a pastry. When she brought them over I asked her how much and – get this – she told me there was no charge. I hadn't really believed the briefing material; but it was true. In Visco, you just walk into a café, and ask for what you want, and it's given to you.

Given. See? I told you it was weird.

Frankly, it just made me even more uncomfortable. I was there to meet with a woman called Dr Farnaby. I'd never met her before, but I'd done the background, obviously, and her profile gave me the creeps. Well, maybe that's not quite right. I think if I met her under normal circumstances I probably wouldn't even give her a second thought.

But these weren't normal circumstances. I mean, my cover story was good – very good – but there was something about Farnaby's profile that made my hands clammy. She didn't, not on paper, at least, look like she should be able to cause me too much trouble – no corporate background, no track record in finance, no history of investment – but the more I read about what she'd been through to get this far, the more I couldn't make it add up. That court case, back at the beginning – imagine! They took on the entire bloody establishment…

Still, whatever miracles they might have pulled off to get it started, it was obvious from the outside that Visco couldn't possibly survive for long without some sort of plug-in to the machine. It's all well and good setting up a radical experiment in sustainable living on an island in the estuary, and it's terribly impressive, sure, to have attracted so many people to give it a go, and the energy systems are amazing and the food solutions are really clever and all that, but, let's face it, they can't build their own electric buses and they can't manufacture the drugs they need and they can't make their own robots so, in the end, they'll still be dependent on the evil capitalist system they think they're running away from.

Which is where I come in. I'm there to offer them money. Quite a lot of money. The cover story is simple. Investors everywhere have noticed what they're up to, and ever since Visco won its court case there have been people all over the world wanting to replicate the model, so there's obviously lots of demand for this sort of thing, and where there's demand there's surely a return. My investors – all of whom have wonderful environmental credentials, and all of whom have very long term perspectives, none of them are in this for a quick buck – want to work with the Visco administration to put the city onto a sustainable footing (in both senses of the word, ha!) and I'm meeting with Dr Farnaby, who sits on the city's finance committee and is close buddies with the chief honcho, to see if we can do some sort of deal.

That's the cover story, anyway. I really was representing a consortium of investors, and they really did have billions available to invest. But in reality, they weren't looking to make a success of Visco and roll it out across the world. Quite the reverse. I'd never met anyone from Statement plc, but they'd pulled it all together, the plan being essentially to undermine the thing from the inside.

Most of the scenarios they'd run showed that Visco was simply catastrophic for the big corporates. For capitalism. They simply couldn't allow it to succeed. Everyone happily getting by with much less stuff, repairing things and making their own food and looking after one another for the sheer joy of it? Where's the profit in that? It just doesn't bear thinking about.

Except, of course, that it was all I could think about, sitting there in that café, waiting for Dr Farnaby. I rehearsed my sales pitch and watched the world going by. None of it made any sense. People were clearly going about their business – young people, old people, people in wheelchairs, people on foot, people of various colours and sizes – but what business were they about? Why did they all look so... so well? Some of the early stuff about Visco reckoned it was like a refugee camp. Now I've never been to a refugee camp but I've seen plenty of them online and on TV and if there's one thing I'm pretty sure of about them is that they're full of people who want to go home.

The people I was looking at didn't look as if they wanted to go home. They looked as if they were already home.

[Miranda]

GOD, IT HAD been such a mad morning. I'd had a meeting with the tech team about the latest rota system, and a call with the designers about the new eco-brewery, and then a meeting with Jo about something or other I can't even remember now, and I'd almost forgotten that I'd agreed to meet this bloke Justin something and as soon as I did remember, I had one of those moments where you go both hot and cold at the same time because, well, you know, it was one of those things you'd agreed to partly because you have to and partly because it was going to be good fun and I couldn't remember where I'd filed the prep so I was almost running from the main office across Paine Square and staring at my screen when I suddenly realised I was heading to the wrong café.

So, yes, I was late.

Still, it probably gave him time to take it all in. They're all the same. It isn't always me that does these meetings, of course, but I probably do more than most. They think we don't know. They get in touch – sometimes it's an email, sometimes a call, sometimes they think of something funky and creative that they think will throw us off the scent, like that time with the guy who wanted to build a vineyard on the south east corner – and they spin some bullshit story about how they want to help or they want to invest or they think they've identified a possible weakness or whatever.

In the beginning we were more naïve – no surprise there – and we'd meet them and listen politely and they'd send the follow-up bumf and we'd have a bit of a think and then someone – usually Daniel, to be fair, and if not him, Jo – one of them anyway – would start to unpick the story and it would slowly dawn on the rest of us and we'd realise that it was just another piece of black ops and whoever had gone to the meeting would feel a mix of shame and anger and would fire off some furious email to tell them where to put their brilliant solution or investment or rescue plan.

That's what I usually did, anyway.

We learned quickly, though. Better than that, I think, we didn't make too many mistakes along the way. Not many of them got through. I don't think we really understood at the beginning just how much of a threat Visco was. To start with we thought – well, I thought – that we were just setting something up that a few people might want to join in with, you know, not exactly a cult but certainly something that only a few weirdos and refuseniks would be interested in. I had no idea that so many people would want to be part of it. That so many people were so pissed off with normal life. And I'd had no idea that so many corporates and politicos and powers-that-be would get so scared so quickly at what was going on.

I still remember how bonkers it was in those first few months. There were literally thousands and thousands of people arriving, it was like a refugee camp, thousands of people who'd had enough of the modern world and who thought that Visco was – was what? The answer? The only available alternative?

Certainly the powers-that-be seemed to think that's what it was – they tried so hard to stop it. And they're still trying.

That's what this guy Justin will be doing. He'll have some cock and bull story about who he represents, and how sincere they are, and how much money they've got and how much they believe in the Visco 'project'. He'll have a nice haircut and a nice suit and, no doubt, the leather on the bottom of his shoes will look like it's only ever seen carpet. Just like all the others, he'll have completely failed to grasp our 'together we're billionaires' strategy. He'll be sitting in front of his coffee and staring out of the window, a quizzical expression on his nervous little face.

I wonder if he'll have seen the poster yet? That's what I was thinking once I was reoriented and heading firmly in the right direction towards the blue café just off Tulip. I wonder if he's seen the poster?

That was why we still went through all this. The obvious thing to do would have been to just start saying no. Once we'd figured out what they were up to, they were easy to spot. We could just as easily have begun refusing the invitations. But we didn't do that. And that, again, is down to Jo and Daniel. And maybe me. I don't know. One day we just seemed to agree: it was better that they came. It was better to let them see it. Most, sure, would leave as cynical as when they'd arrived. But not all of them.

Not all of them. And wasn't that the point of Visco? To show *anyone* that there really was a different way of doing all this?

As I got nearer to the café I could see him through the window, and Linda behind him, and as I got nearer still I could see from the angle of his gaze and the Mona Lisa smile on Linda's face that, yes, he'd seen the poster. The Declaration of Care. Our statement of principles. That simple set of statements, Visco's DNA, working its way into his mind, mysteriously soothing the same doubts and insecurities that he shared with the thousands upon thousands of us already on the island.

'Hello!' I said. 'I'm Dr Farnaby!'

I could see it in his eyes before he even spoke: he'd arrived. He'd found his new home. Now it was simply a question of time.

THE SUSTAINABLE MURDERER

Jenny Curtis

IF SOMEONE HAD told Dylan that morning he would spend his first day of work placement carrying a dead body through Southampton City Centre, he would have told them to pull the other one. But here he was, lugging around a dead guy's diced legs in a duffel bag. That'll be a fun one for when he goes back to school.

Hey, Jamal. How was your week at the city council offices?

Not too bad. What were you up to, Dylan?

Oh, you know, just helping out my contract killer Aunt, the usual.

As if hearing his thoughts, Aunt Becks turned around and flashed him a conspiratorial grin. She was wheeling one of those tartan trolleys you always see old people with. Judging by the left wheel's squeaking and dangerous wobbling, she had probably rescued it from a skip. Dylan silently prayed that the wonky wheel didn't give way, otherwise the man's chopped torso and decapitated head would tumble onto the pavement right outside Westquay Shopping Centre. That would be difficult to explain.

Despite his morals and his mother's voice and the dead weight knocking against his thigh, Dylan returned Becks' smile. The scariest part of work placement so far wasn't the illegality of what he was doing. It wasn't the fact his Aunt had just killed someone in broad daylight and now he was helping carry the body. No, the scariest part was that this was the most fun he'd ever had on work placement.

DYLAN WOULD LIKE to say that he knew something was up the second his Aunt answered the door, but that would be a lie. She just looked like the same Aunt Becks he saw every year on birthdays and at Christmas. Brown bushy hair, the same hooked nose as his mum, and always looking like she had forgotten what she was about to say.

'Dylan!' She pulled him in for a crushing hug, as if his visit was totally unexpected, even though they'd organised this months ago. And his mother had reminded her every week. And Dylan had texted her on his way over this morning. 'Something's come up with a job in town,' she said, finally releasing him. 'Mind if we get started straight away?'

'No, that's cool.' Although Dylan wasn't sure exactly *what* they were getting started on.

'Good, good.' Becks stepped out of the house, locked the door, and walked swiftly down the street. Dylan hurried after her, staring at the tartan trolley she was wheeling along. Yeah, she was old, but she wasn't *that* old. He was pretty sure you needed to be at least sixty to own one of those.

'Mum said to thank you for letting me do work placement with you.'

'It's no problem, anything for my favourite nephew!'

'I'm your only nephew.'

'Hey, tell your mum to drop by sometime,' Becks said, changing the subject with about as much tact as a tap dancing rhino. 'I'm her little sister for Christ's sake. We should, I dunno, get brunch or something.'

They fell into an awkward silence waiting to cross at the roundabout. Well, Dylan was thankful for the silence; it gave him a chance to shove some oxygen down his throat. Aunt Becks must go running or speed walking or *something*. Maybe she did Zumba? Dylan wasn't sure if his Aunt was the sort of person who did Zumba. Actually, he wasn't sure what sort of person she was full stop. He still didn't even know what she did for a living. All he really knew about her was that she was self-employed, lived in a shared house, and made the most awesome carrot cake he had ever tasted.

The traffic cleared and Dylan groaned as Becks practically sprinted across the road.

'So...' she said once her panting nephew managed to catch up. 'How are your GCSEs going? Must be getting close to exam time.'

'I'm in sixth form.'

'Oh.' She broke her stride momentarily. 'Well, how are your A-Levels going then?'

'Okay, I guess.' He shrugged because his mum wasn't here to tell him not to. 'I'm not sure if I wanna go to uni though.'

'Nothing wrong with that. I didn't go to university and I'm doing fine.'

'Yeah, Mum says you run your own company?'

'Something like that,' Becks chuckled to herself.

'Aunt Becks,' Dylan said, deciding to bite the bullet. 'What exactly is it that you do?'

Becks slowed her pace and bit the inside of her cheek, considering her answer. 'You know sustainable farming?' she said.

'Yeah...' Dylan fought the urge to groan. Please don't say he was going to be spending his week *farming*.

'Well, it's nothing like that.'

'Okay, thanks, that's cleared everything up.'

'Look, kid.' Becks stopped abruptly and pulled him over to the side of the path. She lowered her voice to a stage whisper, despite the street being virtually empty.

'Your mum doesn't know what I do, and you *can't* tell her.'

His Aunt let out a breathy laugh just like the one he'd heard his mum use when everything went wrong cooking Christmas dinner.

'I was just gonna take you to the Isle of Wight or something, then bullshit the evaluation, but a job has come up. A big one. And I really need the cash, so I'm taking you with me.' She fixed him with the look that teachers always give you when they ask whether you understand "the seriousness of your actions". 'But before we go you need to know what you're getting into.'

Dylan's head spun. If he was a cartoon character, his eyeballs would be bouncing on springs a foot in front of him. She couldn't be saying what he thought she was saying.

'Are… are you a,' he lowered his voice to match Becks' dramatic whisper, 'prostitute?'

'What? No! Get your mind out of the gutter, boy.' Becks took a deep breath in, pushed her hair back from her face, breathed out. 'I'm a sustainable murderer.'

'A what?'

'You know, like a contract killer?'

'Like in the films?'

'Kind of, except with less spandex, and I make sure that all my jobs are sustainable.'

Dylan hadn't been this confused since he found out

Timbuktu was a real place.

'Right now, in this country, so many resources go to waste,' she explained, her curls bouncing around her head in righteous indignation. 'There's an obsession with consuming, and it's not sustainable. I'm doing my bit to look after the planet.'

'By killing people?'

'No, by *how* I kill people. I always walk or cycle to a job, or take public transport if it's far away. I make sure the clothes and shoes of the target go to someone who needs them. I supplement what food I can with home-grown stuff from my allotment.'

'What does that have to do with killing people?'

'Well, human ashes are a great fertilizer.'

'That's gross!'

'I thought you liked my carrot cake. Besides loads of food is grown in animal shit, and who the hell knows what gets into it in factories?'

'Oh God.' Dylan sat down on the path, head between his knees, trying to remember the grounding exercises his therapist had taught him. *Five senses.*

I can smell car fumes. I can hear seagulls. I can feel the damp from the pavement seeping through my trousers. I can taste bile on the back of my tongue. I can see my Aunt, the sustainable murderer.

'So… you… you *kill* people?'

'Yes, Dylan, I kill people.' A flashy BMW drove past

and someone threw a balled-up McDonald's wrapper out of the window. 'But at least I don't litter like an arsehole!' she yelled after the car. Muttering angrily, she picked up the rubbish and put it in the bin. 'Sorry about that.'

'That's what you're about to do now? You're on your way to kill someone?'

'Yes.' Becks must have seen his apprehension (it would be hard not to) and she crouched down beside him. 'If that bothers you then I can just drop you somewhere in town and pick you up later.'

'No.' The answer seemed to shock both Becks and Dylan. 'Work placement week is meant to be about new experiences.'

'That's the spirit!' Becks beamed and jumped to her feet, holding out a hand to help her nephew up.

'So, where's this target at?'

'Ikea.'

'Ikea?'

'Yeah.' Becks resumed her blister-rubbing, stitch-aggravating pace. 'Ooh! While we're there we should get some of those meatballs, I *love* those! I mean, I probably shouldn't, they're not very sustainable, but I won't tell if you don't.'

She rambled on about meatballs, her mind pinging from one tangent to the next, like a pinball machine of incoherent thoughts. Unlike his Aunt, Dylan's mind was focused. Specifically, on the person he was going to help kill. Who were they? Did they have a partner? A family? What were they buying at Ikea? New tableware for a dinner party? A bookcase for all the books they would never get to read? A cot for their soon to be born child? What had they done to deserve death?

When Dylan tried to ask his Aunt about this, she just shrugged. 'Someone wants him dead and is willing to pay a lot for it. All they sent me was a name, photo, and car reg.'

Becks got the text up on her phone and handed it to Dylan.

Edward Weekes.

White, stocky, brown hair that was rapidly greying, thick wiry eyebrows. He could be anyone. An evil businessman or a Red Cross worker. Dylan hoped for his own sanity he was the former.

They split up in the Ikea carpark to look for the target's car – Becks starting at the top floor and working her way down while Dylan scanned the lower levels. He should have felt apprehensive, should have backed out by now, but instead he felt a disturbing flood of anticipation. His heart was pounding, limbs tingling, breathing erratic. It reminded him of playing spies when he was younger – seeing how far he and his friends could tail someone around town until they caught on. A buzz from his pocket snapped him out of his espionage daze.

White Honda. Top floor.

Dylan closed the text from his Aunt and made his way up the stairs, taking them two at a time. He made a show of sticking close to the walls, edging along then dramatically jumping around corners, all the while singing the *Mission Impossible* theme tune. There was no one around – no Mum telling him to grow up, no friends to look cool in front of, no girls to impress – he could just be himself. And right now being himself involved doing a forward roll across a dirty stairwell floor.

He rounded the corner to the last flight of stairs and saw a man struggling with flat packed furniture. The theme song devolved into a bout of not-so-casual coughing and he resumed walking like a normal person. As he climbed the stairs, the man in front of him attempted to kick open the car park door, but lost his balance and almost toppled over.

'Here, let me get that for you.' Dylan ducked under the flat packed *Liatorp* and held the door open for the man.

'Thanks.' It was only when the man was through the door that Dylan got a good look at his face. The bushy eyebrows. The badger hair. *Edward.* 'You're a life saver.'

There was a quiet *puft* sound. A second later, Edward's jaw went slack, his eyes rolled into the back of his head, and he crumpled to the floor. On the other side of the sprawled body was Aunt Becks holding a blowpipe and grinning manically.

'Good job distracting him, Dylan!' she cheered, then immediately got to work emptying the man's pockets. 'Not a lot of cash, new iPhone, car keys…'

'What's that smell?'

'He shat himself,' Becks said as she tugged the man's jacket off then made quick work of his shirt buttons. 'It's a shame, I'm sure someone would have appreciated those jeans, but never mind. Grab his legs, would you? I think I saw a storage cupboard that I could lop him up in.'

'You're going to cut him up?' Dylan grabbed the man by his ankles, pointedly avoiding his soiled rear, and helped awkwardly shuffle Edward down the stairs. His head lolled like a dog's tongue, arse dragging on every stair as Dylan struggled to support his dead weight.

''Course, makes for easier transportation.'

'So would a car.'

'We can walk it easy. Think sustainably.'

They reached the closet and Dylan let the man's legs fall with a dull thud. Becks opened the closet door and shimmied in backwards, dragging Edward after her.

'Don't worry, you don't have to watch.' She didn't need to look at Dylan's face to know he'd gone green round the edges. 'I know how you are around blood. Good grief, I still remember when your brother cracked his head open playing football. (Keep watch, will ya?)' Becks withdrew a saw, overalls, and a pair of goggles from her bag and closed the closet door. 'He was right as rain, wanted to carry on playing, but you took one look and blew chunks.' Her voice was muffled by the door and the sound of metal sawing through bone.

'So,' Dylan said loudly, trying to block out the ominous cracking from the other side of the door. 'What's the plan? We dumping him in the sea?'

'The sea!' There was a loud crunch that sounded like a limb breaking off. 'Of course we're not going to dump him in the sea! That's littering. Think of the delicate ecosystem.'

Dylan didn't think the ecosystem of Southampton harbour was that delicate. He began to point this out but was interrupted by a thump. That must have been the head coming loose.

'No, we'll take him to my allotment and burn him on a bonfire. Then I'll use the ashes on my soil. It'll be like Bonfire Night, except a month early and without the fireworks.'

If we don't get arrested, Dylan thought. There was no way in hell they'd be able to carry a dead body through the middle of the city without anyone noticing. It couldn't be done. He would screw up somehow. Trip and fall and accidentally fling Edward Weekes' hand at some little old biddy.

But to his astonishment, they didn't get stopped. No one even looked their way twice. It was reassuring in a way. All those times he'd worried about what people thought of him when he walked down the street. Turns out everyone's too preoccupied with their own shit to notice a corpse in a duffel bag, so it's unlikely anyone cares about his haircut or clothes or weight. The realisation put a spring in his step and a swing in his arms, until he remembered he was swinging around a bag of body bits and he stopped abruptly.

'I CAN'T BELIEVE we got away with that!' Dylan whooped as soon as they reached Becks' allotment. 'Holy crap, that was awesome!'

'Calm down, kid. We're not out of the woods yet,' Becks tried to sound stern, but she was grinning too. 'You go grab the camping chairs, I'll start on the fire. Oh, and find some long sticks for these.' She fished a bag of marshmallows out of her trolley and tossed them at him. Dylan caught them on instinct, but held them at arm's length, examining them sceptically.

'Were you keeping these in the same bag as the dead guy?'

'Relax, they're unopened.'

A couple of hours later, the sky was painted pink by the setting sun. The bonfire had shot up and was crackling happily, bright orange flames licking at the dead man's flesh. Dylan poked his marshmallow on a stick into the edge of the fire, watching as it blackened and bubbled like the skin below it. His Aunt sat to his right, eyebrows furrowed and tongue between her teeth as she whittled a piece of wood.

'What you whittling?'

'A blow dart. Used my last one earlier.' She tested the sharpened tip on her finger. 'You see that plant with berries that looks kind of like mistletoe? No, to your left. Over by the greenhouse. Yes, those ones. They're called Doll's Eyes. I use them on my darts, work like a treat. I used to grow them next to my gooseberries but that led to a mix up a couple of years ago. That was a *bad* dinner party, I can tell you…'

Dylan leaned back in his garden chair and allowed himself to take in the evening. Becks' rambling joined the low buzz of flies and the occasional creak and snap of the fire. His fingers were tacky with melted marshmallow goo and he pressed them together, enjoying the resistance as they pulled apart. He felt good. In fact, he felt better than he had in a long time. His anxiety was in check, he was spending a beautiful evening with family, and he'd actually achieved something today rather than sitting around at home or fetching coffee in a stuffy office.

'Aunt Becks?' Dylan interrupted.

'Yeah?'

'Thanks for today. It's been the best.'

'No problem, kid.' Dylan knew she was trying to play it cool, but he could hear the grin in her voice. 'Hey, how about tomorrow I teach you how to make a knife from recycled plastic?'

'Sounds great.' Dylan slouched back into his chair, the metal giving a satisfied creak. This was going to be the best work placement week ever.

ON DAY ZERO

Hanne Larsson

THE SWARTBERG'S JAGGED peaks, behind the karoo plains, are black against the sun rising behind them. There's a wisp or two of cloud, purple and fiery, caressing them, but they are nothing. They won't last beyond the hour after the sun rises, dispersing into pink and orange hues, replaced by a hot and unrelenting blue. Tourists pass through here, thinking the karoo dead space, but there is life. Just slower, adapted, drier. There is beauty in it, most days, and in this silence especially.

It's 5.15 a.m. when Bert de Wet knocks on Susan Burger's door, huddled in a fleece against the morning chill.

'Susie, I want to talk to you. It's important.' His voice is rusty, like the car he turned up in and left at the gate as he wasn't sure the suspension would survive Susie's craggy track down to the house. It's a long walk for a man of Bert's disposition. All of town knows his troubles with his hips. More recently, it's spread to his knees.

'Got nothing to say to you, Bert. Had nothing to say to you for near enough my whole life, so get off my property before I call the police.' There's the sound of metallic rattle from the other side of the door. Bert knows they are the bullets for Susie's shotgun, but he's never feared her.

As legendary as Bert's hips are, the feud between Bert and Susie surpasses this. They're now the only two left alive in Prince Albert who know how it all started. Their fathers were neighbours, and so are they.

'Susie, open the door. Today's Day Zero. We need to talk.'

THE WHOLE WORLD has followed Cape Town's dwindling reservoir stocks, the rationing, the rich boring ever deeper and the price of bottled water increasing with each trip to the supermarket. Bert's seen how the BBC have reported on it; how once again South Africa has made it to their headlines on the internet. Good news never makes it on to the international news pages.

The grey water harvesting, the lack of showers, the reuse of every single drop. It's been an emergency unplanned for and still the sun shines upon the Rainbow Nation as harshly as it ever did. Bert's been watching all the local news from his faded TV set with solidifying worry. This can't go on.

They can't go on like this, and though he's old enough to remember the fights over the water before the timing from the church bells took over, he doesn't want his life to end with this feud hanging over him. Perhaps it's a bit morose, but he doesn't want to die without knowing there's some hope left in the world.

The bolts on Susie's front door slide back, and the door cracks open. Susie's already immaculately turned out, as if she's off to church though he knows she's not set foot in it since her father died and she inherited the feud, alongside the farm. And so Bert knows exactly where she'll be this morning, the same as she is every morning, before her allotted time. He's got about an hour and a half to convince her. He just never imagined she'd look so beautiful to wait for her turn with the water.

'What do I care what happens over that way anyway, de Wet?' Susie's cradling a mug of coffee in her left hand, and the smell of it reminds him that he's not eaten yet. 'They don't care what happens to us out here in the bush, why should I care one whit about their troubles?'

'I don't want us to fight anymore about something neither of us can hardly remember. Our fathers fought, and over what? It's not worth it. Not on Day Zero.'

BERT HASN'T BEEN entirely honest – he remembers quite clearly the story his father drilled into him as they turned the land, planting the crops in their smallholding and waiting for their turn with the lei-water. How Susie's father claimed his watch was correct, when it was slow against Bert's father's, how then his story changed to blaming the gardener, when everyone knew that his gardener had had the day off. His story changed, depending on how many times he recited it, and that was the message Bert's father had given him.

'Can't trust a Burger, son. If they lie about the lei, then what else do they lie about?'

STEALING THE LEIWATER is hard to prove, but the suspicion of it festers. And so it was between them, even when the man from the irrigation board calmly suggested their fathers should put down their spades and set their watches by the church bells. Church chimes have since ensured everyone gets their fair hour.

But here he is, standing outside a Burger's house all the same, wanting to put the suspicion and lies behind them.

'Stay on the veranda. I'll bring some coffee and cake out.' Susie's clipped tone tells Bert all he needs to know. She'll play a good hostess, but he's got a battle on his hands. He thanks her, watching her like a zebra watches a lion pride and stops himself from smiling at her shock over his politeness. She closes the door, but the bolts don't slide back.

Perhaps there's a chance at ending this, after all.

He flops into one of the wicker chairs, his legs and hips too tired to support his weight any longer. The Burgers' veranda is widest as it faces the karoo plains ahead of him, with the mountains along the right side. His view is almost identical though he lives one plot closer into town, one step further in turn for the water, but from this veranda, there's time to take the expanse of it all in. The leiwater runs from the mountains, crisp, clean and free in channels alongside Prince Albert's roads, held in by sluice gates and furrows. It's precious, and never once has the lei run dry.

But what with the issues in Cape Town, perhaps one day it could. And then what will become of the town? Will everyone feud? He must end this, if only to prove to everyone that peace can be found even among uncertainty.

He can smell the aridness of the karoo from here, though at this time in the morning, it smells faintly of his grandmother's herb garden. When the sun gains height, all you'll smell is dust.

Susie opens the door, but Bert resists the urge to help her. It's an unfair likeness, he knows, but she reminds him of a skittish horse. Ignoring them and letting them come to you is the best thing to gain their trust, and so that's what he does, sitting there, facing the oncoming morning.

'Milk, sugar?'

He responds, but there must have been some mix-up in what he says because the mug he's offered has a dash of milk and is bitter when he asked for sweet and black. He swallows, picking out a slice of the cake she offers him, thanking her at each sip and bite. He tries not to study her, but can't help himself, and becomes acutely aware of his gnarly, browned face against her pale porcelain skin. Her hands at least show signs of hard work, but still look delicate compared to his huge calloused ones.

'Well, you wanted to talk but here you are, eating my cake and drinking my coffee without saying a word. Spit it out, my hour's nearly here.' She looks flustered now, and Bert's sorry for it. He wonders how to begin to undo half a century and more of griping and snide and underhandedness with one cup of coffee and a mention of Day Zero.

'Do you not worry our water will run out one day, Susie?'

Bert glances at her then, watches as her gaze slips away from him, back to her mug and then out over the vast bush before them. Once, they were friends, playing in the water runnels, kicking a ball, or out in the bush picking karoo plants for his grandmother's many potions. If a nation could try to learn to forgive each other, surely two people could do the same. He watches her inhale, deeply, eyes closed, as if she's breathing in the silence.

'Some days. But we have a system. It works. We're different here.' Susie almost spits out the words, as if she and the city also have some long-standing disagreement. Perhaps they do, Bert isn't too sure, but Susie only moved back from somewhere else when her father got sick. Whereas Bert never left. His ex-wife did, a long time back, and in all honesty, he can't say he misses her. Bert knows he's in love with Susie in a way that he was never in love with his wife. He cared for her, of course, but what he feels for Susie seems as certain as saying that each day will be sunny and clear skies, or as overwhelming to the senses as when the karoo blossoms and becomes a green carpet after rain. Its intermittent, unpredictable beauty leaves you gasping when it shows. And Day Zero has brought it all crashing in on him. He wants Susie to know all this.

'If you're just going to sit on my veranda in silence, Bert, you could just as easy go home and do so. I've got my day to be getting on with.' Susie's voice still has a hard edge to it. He's been remiss in not explaining more about why he's come.

'Sorry, I was just trying to find the right words to say why I'm here. I thought I'd planned it all out in my head, but now I've come it seems a bit stupid.' He stops, but Susie has leant back in her chair, showing no signs of moving, and he's emboldened by this. 'I've been watching the news, and I think the irrigation board should do more to stop the water being wasted. We humans are to blame. Are we killing the karoo?'

'So take it up with them, then,' Susie retorts, helping herself to a slice of cake. '*Why* are you here, Bert?'

'Because I don't want to leave this world without knowing there's hope left in it, or that we helped protect what we live in. Because our fathers' feud ate at us both, and I'm tired of it. Cape Town is just the start – they're already fighting over the water, and our families have festered over watches either being too fast or too slow, but we've always had it. What if the lei runs dry? What humanity will we have left then if we fight over such a stupid thing as time now?' Bert's breathing is loud in his ears as he lapses back to the silence. He watches her take a sip of the coffee, can feel her gaze assessing the truth of his words.

'Fair words, Bert, but I can't help but think there's something else.' Susie has crooked one eyebrow at him over the rim of her mug, and suddenly it's like they are ten years old again and she's caught him trying to copy her answers on their maths test. Bert blushes, the heat of it creeping down his neck, and Susie chuckles at this silent admission of guilt.

'Because I'm in love with you,' he whispers, 'and I think I always have been. Because every day we carry on, a further part of me shrivels like Grandmama's drying plants.'

He doesn't dare look at her; instead he focuses his gaze on her neatly laid out rows of planting, of how the bees have started to flock to the lavender and where the proteas mingle with the roses and the marrows. In the distance, he hears the cough and splutter of Miss Katy's car engine. It is, after all, a weekday, and town will be busy soon enough. He should be getting on with his day and leaving Susie to hers.

'And what happens tomorrow then, on Day One?' she asks, breaking the quiet of a morning that had settled around them like a worn coat. Bert's at first not sure he's heard her, what with his hearing aid and the thoughts buzzing in his head.

'I'll stop by for coffee again, if you'll have me.' Bert smiles as he says this, but doesn't dare laugh, afraid that any sudden sounds will break this fragile thing they've established in the growing morning heat. Skittish horses and all that.

The church bells chime, and they listen to them count to six, announcing Joseph's hour. Susie's is next, then Bert's. Water for everyone.

'Some things change, and some things remain the same. Come check the furrows with me,' Susie states, rising from her chair, and Bert knows it's not an offer lightly made. 'Perhaps next time you offer me coffee?'

JUST IN CASE

Rose Krawczuk

THE MAN IN the grey anorak stood at the mahogany counter. Behind him, sitting quietly on worn mismatched sofas and chairs, twenty or so customers clutched small red tickets that dictated when they could approach the desk. The man looked down at the old lady beyond the counter and sighed. She never made it easy.

'Well, says here you ordered a pair of hedge trimmers.' Her ancient voice had the scratchy quivering quality of someone who had outstayed their welcome in life.

The man took a deep breath. The air in the reception room tasted musty, as if it was still clinging to its library roots, grasping at the scent of the old books that used to line its walls. Steps on either side of the vast counter led up to a stone gallery, backed by two massive wooden doors. Of course, the whole thing was simply a facade now and the old lady was just one small part of it. In fact, the only indication of the building's current purpose could be found in the square metal hatch behind the counter, which occasionally spat items onto a black conveyor belt. The man flinched as the hatch screeched open. For a fraction of a second, he could see into the great silver warehouse and hear the robots whizzing around, replacing returned items on shelves and collecting new ones for the conveyor.

The old lady winced and groaned at the racket as she pressed her hands theatrically over both ears. The hatch banged closed and she looked up at the man from behind her tortoiseshell glasses, pushing them up to the top of her nose with her little finger. Their magnification was so strong that her dark green eyes consumed each lens. The man had seen that furrowed brow and turned-down mouth so many times before. It was going to be a bumpy ride.

'That's the problem, I actually ordered a pair of heavy-duty secateurs.'

'Well, I just leant out the last pair of those so there's nothing I can do about that.' She spoke in a loud whisper, as if it were still a library. Her gaze returned to the computer screen.

'You should have double-checked what you entered, just in case. Please bring back the hedge-trimmers tomorrow.'

A wave of anger washed over him and his face began to heat up. He hated it when people dismissed him. He went out of his way to be polite, but this woman tore at the very fabric of his morality.

'But I don't want the hedge-trimmers!' he cried.

The old lady met the man's incredulous gaze, her glasses teetering once again on the end of her nose. She pointed at a propped up sign on the far end of the counter that featured the profile of a woman with a finger to her lips and read, *Please keep your voice down in the library.*

'Well, you must take the hedge-trimmers otherwise it will ruin the whole system. Bring them back tomorrow, please.' The woman rose from her seat and shuffled over to the back of the reception, the soles of her feet squeaking on the shiny parquet floor, where she busied herself with precarious stacks of yellowing paper. The man stood rooted to the spot, his mouth moving but no words coming out. He yearned to reason with her but deep down he knew she'd always win the fight. It just wasn't worth it. Instead, he took a deep breath and picked up the hedge-trimmers. He was about to leave when the woman called over to him.

'If you could fill in one of these sheets before you go, please.'

'What is it?' His voice quivered. 'Just a questionnaire about the computer system. Feel free to criticise its incompetence on this occasion... just in case.' She mumbled the last few words under her breath as she placed the sheet on the countertop and pushed it slowly towards him. The fingernails of her wrinkled hands were long and sharp and red and reminded the man of the Wiccan horror films his friends had made him watch as a child. The form glided right over the polished surface and landed on the floor in front of him. He eyed her suspiciously.

'Errm, I'll fill that out online when I have a bit more time. Thanks.' The act of disagreeing with her unleashed a sensation of power inside him. Needless to say, it didn't last long.

'Well, there is no online form for this. Just sit down there and fill this out before you leave, please.' A commanding finger pointed towards an uncomfortable Chesterfield sofa behind him.

The man stared at her, his eyes wide, but she turned away and stared at the computer screen. The sickly smell of the old lady's rosewater perfume transported him back to his childhood. Before the sharing revolution, the rooms behind the ornate wooden doors were packed full of books. When the library was converted, they were removed to make way for a colossal metallic warehouse, containing all sorts of different items that people used to store in their cupboards, sheds and attics, only taking them out once in a blue moon. People used to be so frivolous. His own parents were frivolous. Millions of lawnmowers and vacuum cleaners rolled off production lines so that everybody could have their own – just in case. It seemed so obvious now that sharing was the better solution, it's a wonder it took so long to realise. Well, of course, we'd been doing it with books and graduation robes for donkey's years now, but why those items should have been singled out, he just didn't know.

The man grabbed the paper from the floor and snatched a pen from the counter. Her stern gaze forced him to regret his passive-aggressive manner.

He perched on the edge of the sofa; he had fond memories of this seat. As a teenager he once snuck into the library late at night with his high-school girlfriend. It was a rite of passage, tiptoeing around the pitch-black rooms, scouring for evidence that the librarian was actually a witch. Nobody ever found anything, of course. When they'd returned to the reception hall, his girlfriend pulled him down onto the uncomfortable red leather sofa, where they fooled around until the caretaker shone a bright light in their faces and asked them to leave. The pair of them ran home in fits of laughter, rolling around in the grass on the heath. It had been a long time since he'd had so much fun with a girlfriend.

He held the yellowing sheet in front of him. It was slapdash: badly formatted and littered with spelling errors. He looked up at the woman again. Had she created this fake form herself? He put these thoughts to the back of his mind and filled it in to avoid further disagreement. Then he returned to the desk and handed it back to her. Without taking her eyes from her computer screen, she slipped the form off the top of the counter and perused the document.

For the second time that day the man lingered in front of the desk, watching the old lady's finger draw a thin red line down the form as her nail varnish rubbed away. What should he do now? Was he allowed to leave yet? When she finished reading the document she returned her attention to the screen, wrinkling her nose to adjust her glasses. The clock ticked conspicuously. Distant clunking noises sounded behind the wall.

'Yes? What is it now?' she said sharply when she real-ised the man was still there.

'Errm… Is that OK? Can I go now?' He blushed.

'Yes, I suppose I can work with this,' she said, shaking the paper in the air with one hand.

'Please leave and close the door behind you… And don't forget the hedge-trimmers!'

AS THE DOOR was closing the old lady looked up from the desk, pushing her tortoiseshell spectacles slowly to the top of her nose. She waited until the latch clicked shut, just in case, then she looked around the room at all the other customers, some yawning, others absorbed by their phones. They been waiting there for a long time already, what harm would ten more minutes do? She turned her focus to the computer screen. What had this man been borrowing lately? He was always in here; always wanting something of hers.

You could learn a lot about a person by studying their borrowing history, she mused. For instance, a desire for a lawnmower suggested they had a garden. A regular borrower of toys probably had children or grand-children. And a person with a preference for books or laptops over chairs and wine glasses was likely an introvert. But it was the time-wasters that really piqued her interest…

The old lady hated the time-wasters. She actively took pride in her record of pushing them onto the next library where the cheerful and helpful custodian, Graham, could deal with them. It was wrong for a custodian to be so cheerful, she thought, but he'll learn. The old lady paused for a second. Recently she'd heard about a trial library that had dispensed with human staff altogether. She dismissed the idea; robots were idiots, in her opinion. Twisting herself around in her chair, she smirked at the piles of yellowing forms filled out by irritated customers. It was all part of the campaign against the incompetency of the computer system that she had been working on ever since she found out. At least I won't be replaced by robots, she chuckled to herself.

The old lady continued to pry into the man's records: protective clothing, paint brushes, power cleaners, board games, retro video game consoles, six plates, six wine glasses. She investigated the borrowing history of each item. Curious. Very curious indeed. A second name seemed to be popping up everywhere: Elodie James. The two had been borrowing exactly the same items, at very similar times. Intriguing.

'House-proud and sociable,' she murmured. There should be no need for two borrowers to check out the same items like this. A plan was forming. The potential increase in efficiency was exhilarating. She searched for the other borrower in the database.

'Yes!' she exclaimed. This Elodie woman was currently borrowing a pair of heavy-duty secateurs. The old lady decided to perform an immediate recall of the item, designating a time slot of between twelve and one o'clock tomorrow. She carried out the same process for the man with the hedge-trimmers and sat back, smiling to herself, before beckoning the next unsuspecting customer to the counter.

THE FOLLOWING DAY, a secateur-wielding woman arrived at around twelve o'clock. She burst through the door, almost smashing it into the wooden panelling, then strode over to the reception desk. The old lady behind the counter was the only other sign of life in the room, and even that was questionable. It was an odd time to recall an item. The woman shrugged her shoulders as if she'd been conversing out loud, then leaned casually on the counter, running one nonchalant hand through her wavy black hair. 'I have an item to return.'

The old lady pottered around before answering, neatening piles of paper and straightening lines of pens and pencils. A knowing smile appeared on the black-haired woman's mouth. The old crone was up to her usual tricks.

'Sit down over there, please.'

'Your wish is my command…' The woman wandered over to a sun-bleached chaise. Loud machinery rattled and the conveyor started up, swallowing a number of poorly stacked boxes that threatened to topple onto the floor. There was a crash on the other side of the hatch and the old woman mumbled something about the idiot machines, picking up a yellowing form and scribbling furiously on its dusty surface, a curious malicious smile on her face. The woman's eyes narrowed as she wondered whether the old lady purposefully made life difficult for the poor machines as well as the borrowers.

After a while, the woman slunk into the dusty uncomfortable chair and got out her phone. If experience was anything to go by she could be in for a long wait.

AT AROUND ONE o'clock, the old lady watched as the heavy wooden door opened tentatively and the man in the grey anorak stepped in, flustered, rain-soaked and out of breath. He pressed the door closed behind him and wandered towards the counter, his wet feet slipping across the shiny wooden floor. The old lady pointed to a seat next to the woman and the man paused for a second, his eyes widening as he noticed the pair of heavy-duty secateurs in her hands. The old lady scrutinised the scene: the man's mouth opening and closing but no sound coming out. She'd need to work some magic.

'Paul, please come up to the counter.' The old lady had only discovered his name this afternoon after twenty years of interaction – using it was all part of the plan.

'Umm… But this woman was here before me…' Paul stole a glance in the black-haired woman's direction and hesitated, half on and half off the sun-bleached chaise.

Step one: man interacts with woman.

'Thanks for your input, Paul, but I am in charge of when I see the customers. Come up to the counter, please.' She smirked slyly to herself, straightening her back.

As he dragged himself up to the counter he flashed a meek apologetic smile at the black-haired woman, who winked overtly in response.

Step two: man and woman strike up an allegiance.

The old lady tried to look severe and was surprised to find it was hard when she had to try.

'Please place the item on the counter.' She knocked on the wood, which gave out a hollow, empty sound.

'But I already have!' Paul exclaimed, pulling down the

skin of his cheeks in despair. The old lady chose to ignore this.

'I can see you've ordered another item. A pair of heavy-duty secateurs. These are not yet in stock. Please come back tomorrow.'

Paul looked at her with wild, crazy eyes.

'But this woman has a pair to return!' He gestured to the woman who threw her head back and burst into fits of laughter, her voice rebounding off the hard stone and wood. She stuffed a hand over her wide mouth, feigning a cough. When she seemed to have regained her composure, she strode over to the counter.

'Yes, I'm happy to return these so that... Paul, is it? Can take them out right away.' The woman smiled intently at Paul, then added, 'I'm Elodie, by the way.'

Step three: man and woman on first name basis.

He looked at her fondly for a brief second and then stared at his shoes. Nostalgia hit the old lady like a jolt of electricity. She recalled Harry standing right at that spot all those years ago, staring at his feet as he asked her out for dinner. All that afternoon he had been peeking at her from across the study area, the diffuse light from the orange desk lamp giving his face a soft angelic glow. The memory was so exhilarating that she found herself sharing in the borrowers' elation. She hadn't expected this to happen.

'Well, excuse me, but I set the rules here,' the old lady

crowed. She gazed blankly at Elodie and pushed the unruly glasses to the top of her nose. She was consciously trying to behave as normal as possible, despite an unmistakable rush of excitement.

'Elodie. We just need to go through your recent borrowing history. Just in case...' She trailed off and looked on furtively as Elodie rolled her dark eyes dramatically at Paul. His cheeks bloomed and he put a thin, elegant hand to his mouth to hide a smile.

The old lady scrolled through the page she had set up as a prop. She couldn't forget the records if she tried. Behind the hatch there was a muffled beeping noise that threatened to distract her – those damned robots again. Not today, she had much more important work to do. She smiled to herself. 'Protective clothing, paint brushes, power cleaners, board games, retro video game consoles, six plates, six wine glasses...'

'Well that's the same as my borrowing history!' His sudden exclamation seemed to have surprised him as much as anybody else. His face fell. 'Perhaps you're looking at the wrong records?'

'Excuse me but I am never looking at the wrong records.'

Elodie looked amused as Paul winced at the old lady's ferocity.

'She's right. That's my borrowing history.' She flitted her eyes flirtatiously at Paul. He was gazing intently at her, his mouth flickering with the beginnings of a smile, the nervous wrinkles on his forehead loosening. All evidence of his shyness seemed to have dissolved.

Step three: man and woman find out just how much they have in common.

The old lady let the room fall into silence while the borrowers considered one another, thoughtfully. After a while, Elodie spoke to the old lady, not once taking her eyes from Paul.

'I think I'll reorder the secateurs for another day, if that's OK?' She winked at Paul.

The old lady was astute enough to spot a conspiracy. Under ordinary circumstances, she would find this kind of flouting of the rules abhorrent. It is absolutely out of the question to share borrowed items between people at different addresses. In short, it made a mockery of the whole system… But she'd let it slide, she thought, just this once.

As they exited the room, the old lady heard Paul mumble something about coffee. Elodie nodded vigorously. There was a cheerful sound of receding laughter as they crossed the threshold, then silence as the door shut behind them.

Step four: man and woman make plans together.

Decades of stiffness in the old lady's body melted away. To unite two borrowers a noble cause, an efficiency she just couldn't resist. As she considered the two lovers, Harry popped into her mind again. She couldn't bring him back, she lamented, but she might be able to bring others together.

THAT AFTERNOON, THE old lady whiled away the time between customers tracking her own borrowing history. Just in case.

TRUCE

Emily Hibbs

IT WAS ALWAYS a toss-up, whether to bargain first with the sea or the sky. Above, a bruising of clouds chased the sun towards the western horizon. Below, the waves sized each other up, spitting icy spray onto the deck. More time, Nadia pleaded from the back deck of *Endurance.* Give us more time. The landscape was painted with a grey wash that could only be called daylight in the loosest sense, and the skipper's half-hourly update on tomorrow's storm forecast did little to help the crew's morale – or Nadia's concentration. The party chief forced her frozen fingers back to the task of reassembling the faulty equipment, piece by piece.

Finally, she beckoned the others over. Their hands darted over the cables and secured the magnetometer in place, before the group winched it into the water. They stood gathered on the deck, their hi-vis jackets flapping in the wind, a cluster of beacons in the greyness. As the mag was lowered to the right depth, Nadia studied the monitor, her eyes darting across the dancing lines of data on the screen. A breath she didn't know she'd been holding in whistled through her lips. She clapped her second on the shoulder.

'Try to finish the line,' she told Jack.

'Roger that,' he replied with a smile, but the three thin creases on his forehead showed no sign of disappearing.

One crease for every set back. Two sensor malfunctions and a storm forecast. It was almost as if the world didn't want them to save it.

Nadia dragged her aching legs down into the hold. Back in her cabin, she wiped the salt crust from her eyelashes before falling onto her bunk, still in her overalls. Unless their fortunes changed dramatically – and quickly – they were not going to make the survey deadline. Not only did that mean at least another week at sea, but Nadia would also miss the company-chartered plane back to England. It would be another month until the next WorldWind flight home; another month in lonely hotel rooms far from everyone she knew and loved. There was no way she'd have enough CarbonCreds to buy her own ticket for a commercial airline, even if there were any scheduled.

The limited data they'd collected didn't even flag any potential unexploded ordnance sleeping beneath the seabed. The Climate Wars had left most of these humble fishing towns alone; but further south, mines were scattered like deadly seeds. There was always the chance though of a stray reaching these northern waters. And like dogs, stray bombs were often the most unpredictable. Of course, if the seabed was clear, this was good news for the next stage of the project; the engineers could get to work on building the turbines, raising a thousand more masts in the ocean. But that didn't make her feel any better about being here, conducting a seemingly pointless survey.

The boat rolled over the waves, and Nadia's stomach rolled with it. The best thing to do is sleep. This was the first thing she'd learned on her first trip offshore. The first thing she now told the newcomers. When seasickness comes calling, close your eyes and sink into oblivion until it gives up and goes away. She settled into the thin mattress, and let her eyelids droop. Her mind drifted south, weaving between the wind farms, navigating the North Sea until it reached the Thames estuary, where it floated up the river, past the car cemetery at Canvey Island, the sky farms of Canary Wharf, the Houses of Parliament at Westminster, all the way to the little flat in West London. A smile slid across her face as she imagined her mother peeling sweet potatoes in the kitchen, her little brother Nat washing tomatoes beside her, their cohabiter Mister Thomas picking herbs on the balcony. She tried to recall the fresh aroma of mint, the lemony scent of coriander, but the damp metallic smell of the cabin overpowered her memories. She fell asleep with her stomach aching for home. Above, the clouds held an urgent meeting. Below, the waves tussled.

THE NEXT MORNING, Nadia had barely been out on deck an hour when more bad news arrived. It came in the form of five black marks on the horizon, spaced evenly apart like neat stitches sewing sky to sea.

'We've got company,' Nadia told her team. Jack straightened, peered over the stern and spotted the boats. It was a familiar if unwelcome sight, and they saw it on nearly every survey; the fishermen of the village had become tired of waiting again.

'Do you want me to call Eirik?' he asked. Their fisherman go-between was responsible for keeping the others in check, convincing them to steer clear of Endurance's path while the area was being surveyed – a task made somewhat easier by a generous reimbursement from WorldWind.

Nadia shrugged. 'There's not much he can do if they're already here. Just collect as much data as you can before they disrupt the line. Storm's nearly on us anyway.'

An hour later, the fishing boats had settled stubbornly in *Endurance's* path and cast their nets over the side. Nadia frowned as she recognised the boat furthest away –

egg-yolk yellow with a red stripe. Eirik wasn't in to answer his phone, anyway.

The clouds relieved themselves with a sigh of rain as Nadia and Jack winched up the magnetometers and packed them away. As the wind began to blow in earnest, the captain set a course for the port.

Once onshore, the crew trudged off towards one of the bars on the far side of the little town, the one they had nicknamed 'The Vennlig'. The Friendly. Nadia stayed on board, waiting for the fishing boats to return. The waves were slapping over the harbour decking by the time they sailed in.

'God dag, Eirik,' Nadia called out as the last figure disembarked.

Eirik squinted up through the hammering rain and, spotting her, raised a hand in acknowledgement.

'Can we speak?' Nadia asked. Eirik cast his head about, and for a moment Nadia thought he was shaking it in outright refusal, but then he pointed at a sheltered hut. Neutral ground. Tucking her braids into her hood, Nadia walked down the ramp to the shelter, the rain buffeting the exposed skin of her face. The older man took off his hat and watched her coolly. The creases around his eyes reminded her of the ever-laughing Mister Thomas, but Eirik rarely had a smile for anyone working for World-Wind.

'We offered you and the other fishermen reimbursement,' Nadia started. She had learned from experience that it was better to be direct. 'We asked you not to disrupt the survey.'

Eirik held out his hands. 'It was not enough. They wanted to fish.'

'And you wanted to go with them?' Nadia asked, her eyebrow twitching. Eirik was supposed to be on their side.

'If they fish, then I fish. Otherwise, those that they supply are satisfied, and those that I supply are not.'

'We can offer more money,' said Nadia.

'It is not money that they want,' Eirik replied.

'We have no more CarbonCreds,' said Nadia, folding her arms. The CarbonCred argument was familiar ground. Nadia had enough company pride to be ashamed of the WorldWind carbon score. Their goal was to power projects using one hundred per cent renewable energy, while working towards a world where 'renewable energy' was synonymous with 'energy'. Yet still, their carbon score remained relatively high, their credits used to pay off the fishing villages whose livelihoods the new wind farms threatened.

'Then they will fish,' said Eirik, his shoulders heaving up into a shrug. 'What are we supposed to do? We're walled in from the east with one farm, from the west with another. Soon you will leave, and your colleagues will come and build one right on our doorstep. Where can we fish then? Nowhere.'

So don't fish! Nadia wanted to shout at him. She pressed her lips tightly together, until the words released their pressure on her tongue. She knew it was an entitled thing to think. How could a twenty-something from London – raised without the taste of anything with a face passing her lips, the opportunities of an environmentally-minded metropolis at her fingertips – assume to reprimand this man almost three times her age? Eirik and his peers followed in the wake of their mothers, fathers and grandparents. This town was built on fish, and the slippery foundations were beginning to rot. Those living on the mound could only watch, wide-eyed, as everything they knew was taken from them by an army of towering turbines. And why? Their forebears had not taken more than their due. They were not the ones that had built towering factories, puffing poison into the air, nor were they the ones who had cut down their forests for toxic beef farms. They weren't even the ones who had dredged the life out of the southern seas with trawlers. They lived quietly, setting their feet in the footholds of their ancestors.

They were both fighting the same battle, trying to protect a fading world they loved.

'If you don't mind –' Eirik pulled his hat back on over his thunder-cloud hair – 'I'd like to get back. My granddaughter is visiting from Paris.'

Nadia watched him walk across the decking and into

the town, until she lost sight of him among the neat red houses, their windows shuttered against the encroaching weather. She set off for The Vennlig, her posture tense, her mind dancing with doubts.

Seated at a table in the corner of the bar, the water sliding off her jacket into a puddle on the floor, Nadia tried to pay attention to the team's conversation. But her mind kept wandering outside to the storm, to the fishermen and women in their homes… She wrapped her hands around her glass of orange juice and breathed it in. The smell of oranges always reminded her of Mister Thomas and of home. He had moved in when she was just seven years old, the first of her friends whose family signed up to the cohabit initiative. She'd been scared at first, of this big, old man – he was old even then – who had taken a room in their home, bringing with him a bundle of plants to grow on the balcony and a bow-tie collection in a box that looked like a treasure chest.

'There are too many people trying to fit in this city,' her mother had told her. 'And we have a spare bedroom.'

One day she had watched him from beneath the kitchen table, singing to their little orange tree. *If I call the sun, will you fruit for me? If I call the sun, will you be happy?* She was too timid to join in, but when he left to collect his morning newspaper, she'd snuck out and whispered the words to the plant. The sweet citrus smell had captivated her, and she found she wasn't afraid of

Mister Thomas anymore. A couple of years later, on a night she'd never forget, his eyes were full of stars as he told her about the Climate Wars. His voice hummed with emotion as he spoke of the threateningly firm handshakes, the compulsory evacuations, a cloud blooming into a mushroom on the horizon, three cities in three countries struck off the map. But then, when the world dangled over a precipice – the armistice. She begged him to tell her more about the clearances, the rebuilding, the endless initiatives. The rest she knew. CarbonCreds were introduced to limit the amount of harmful products and services people could buy or use. Cars too inefficient to drive were abandoned across the country, rusting in mass graves. Commercial flight tickets became the domain of the very wealthy, or the very carbon-frugal. And every-where solar, wind, hydro. Slowly, the Earth began to heal.

A stab of homesickness hit her, so sharp that she thought she might cry out with the pain of it. We are building something bigger than me, bigger than home, she reminded herself. We are fixing what we broke. She took a sip of her orange juice, and laughed along with a joke she'd been too distracted to hear the punchline of.

AN HOUR LATER, Nadia began to make her excuses. She carried her glass over to the counter. Behind the bar, the back door was open, rain throwing itself onto the floor through the gap. The barman stood in the doorway, leaning down to speak to someone at the bottom of the steps. The wind carried away most of the conversation, but Nadia caught a word she recognised, the sound of it like hail pattering on a roof; *datterdatter*. Eirik stepped into the bar, his face a mess of rain and anguish. Catching sight of Nadia, his flurry of words switched from Norwegian to English.

'Please, have you seen a little girl? My granddaughter is missing. She's wearing her blue coat, dark blue. She's nine years old. Her hair grows to here –' he placed a hand, palm side down, on his shoulder. 'She disappeared about an hour ago, one minute, sitting in the kitchen, the next...'

He trailed off, his gaze flicking around the inn, as if his granddaughter might crawl out from under a table, or peek from behind a curtain.

'I haven't seen her,' Nadia said gently. 'We've all been in here for a few hours.'

Eirik lifted the bar hatch and strode over to consult the survey and vessel crew around the table. Before they had finished shaking their heads, he was already walking towards the exit.

Nadia caught the door as it swung to close.

'I'll help you look,' she said simply. 'What's your granddaughter's name?'

Eirik stared at her for a moment.

'Aubrey,' he said finally.

Nadia nodded. She fastened her jacket, the zip digging into her neck, and pulled the hood over her head. Eirik didn't look back as he headed towards the harbour, bowed against the wind. Nadia followed behind, splitting off every now and again to search the adjacent roads, squinting through the shards of rain for a pale face. Seeing Eirik's stony features transformed by fear had ignited something in Nadia. It had reminded her that people were people.

By the time they'd reached the shore, the sea and the sky were raging against each other. Twenty-foot high waves arched their back and leaped towards the heavens. The clouds rumbled, retaliating with sharp stabs of lightning. The boats in the harbour jostled, caught in the middle of the conflict. Nadia walked along the decking, almost losing her footing as a swell broke across her path.

'Aubrey!' Eirik called out again and again, the wind snatching away his words as soon as they were set lose. No small figure appeared.

Rat-ta-ta-ta-ta.

Nadia looked around, searching for the source of the noise too rhythmic to be rain. A face was pressed against the cabin window of one of the fishing boats, wide eyes framed by strings of dark hair. The girl tapped on the window again. Eirik yelped as he spotted his granddaughter. They scrambled across the decking, barely keeping their footing on the slippery surface. They saw that the storm must have dislodged several coils of rope, sending them sliding down the deck to pile in front of the cabin, their weight too heavy for Eirik's granddaughter to open the door. Nadia and Eirik lowered themselves onto the deck as the boat jogged and bucked on the rough sea. Heaving the loops of rope away from the door, the fisherman and the party chief cleared a space. Aubrey pushed the door open, shivering, her eyes fixed meekly on the deck. Even the storm seemed to quieten for a moment as the clouds took a breath and the waves shushed each other.

'Papy,' she said breathlessly. 'I'm sorry. I came to the boat, but then the rain was so heavy, and there was a crash and I couldn't get out—'

Eirik wrapped his arms around her. 'But why were you here in the first place?'

It was hard to tell in the twilight, but Nadia thought Aubrey's cheeks flushed. She looked sheepish as Eirik stroked her damp hair, flattening it to her head.

'Come,' he told her. Eirik turned to Nadia, jerking his head back towards the village, his eyebrows raised with an unspoken question. With a nod, Nadia followed the pair back to Eirik's home.

Steam swirled off her clothes as Nadia sat beside the hearth, rubbing her soaking feet into the rug, a little guiltily. The hushed conversation in the hallway continued. Nadia let her head sink onto her chest and watched the drops hitting the window. The rain was falling with less vigour now, as if the clouds' hearts weren't in it. The whispers stopped, and Nadia heard light footsteps as Aubrey padded away down the hall.

'Well,' said the fisherman, coming into the living room. 'She was trying to sink my boat.'

Nadia set her fragrant mug of warm tea on a side table and stared at him. A twitch ticked at the corner of Eirik's mouth; Nadia wondered if he was attempting to rein in his anger in front of her, before she realised he was suppressing a smile.

'We were talking about the ... disagreement. The surveys; the turbines. She argued with me a bit, but then she went quiet – I thought she was just tired. Turns out she was mutinous. She must have slipped out while I was cooking dinner.'

'What did she plan on doing?' Nadia asked, trying to school the shock in her voice.

'I don't think she'd thought that far ahead. She took a hammer – perhaps she was going to try and bash a hole in the bottom.'

Nadia felt her eyebrows shoot up to her hairline.

'I wouldn't have done it,' said a small voice, coloured with a French accent. Aubrey stood in the doorway, wrapped in a dressing gown, her hair towel-tussled. But she sounded unsure. Eirik looked from his granddaughter's uncertain expression, to Nadia's, and the lip twitch flickered again. A smile spread across the fisherman's face and he gave a laugh that was half roar.

'WorldWind is the future,' said Aubrey seriously, reciting the advert with perfect inflection. Nadia picked up her mug again, holding it in front of her lips to hide her smile.

'No,' Eirik said, reigning in his laughter. 'You are the future.'

Aubrey thanked Nadia shyly, and then kissed her grandfather goodnight. Eirik stared at the place his granddaughter had been standing, wearing an expression that was neither frown, nor smile, but had elements of both.

'When I last saw her, she was only up to the back of your chair. These children, they grow faster than beansprouts,' he said with a sigh. 'The flights from France are just too expensive – the amount of CarbonCreds is completely unreasonable. My daughter could not even come with her this time.' He shook his head. Nadia took a last gulp of tea and stood up to leave. Eirik rose too, and reached out a hand. They shook, meeting each other's eyes for the briefest instant. He walked her to the door.

'The rain has stopped,' he said quietly as they stood on the threshold. Then, 'I will speak to the others again. Ask them to rest tomorrow. The next day – who can say?'

He shrugged in that way of his that Nadia had come

to be familiar with. The shrug of a man who knew the limits of his sphere of influence, and had no wish to expand them. Nadia waved, and set off down the path to the harbour.

THE NEXT MORNING, the clouds flew their white flags. The waves rolled onto the shore, whispering in with a *whish* and out with a *truce*. Below the seabed in the shadow of a ship, a sea mine waited for its magnetic field to give up the decades long game of hide-and-seek. On board, the party chief caught the scent of oranges, blowing on the sea breeze.

The following two stories were originally published in the cli-fi anthology, *Nothing Is As It Was*, published by Retreat West Books on Earth Day 2018 to raise funds for the Earth Day Network.

They were used in research by Dr Denise Baden at the University of Southampton as to what kinds of stories inspire more sustainable behaviour. The results showed that it's feel-good, hopeful stories that make people more inclined to change their ways.

BLUE PLANET COLLECTION
Jane Roberts

LITTLE DAVID WATCHES Big David on the television screen, listens with gaping seashell ears every single week. Together, they dive into the blue universe beyond. Without the inconvenience of the seagrass matting in the lounge becoming flooded with salt water. Details like these bother Little David's mother. Other details too, such as: when had the fish tank become so...bare? Somehow the three tropical inhabitants appear more prominent.

'Daaaaav-id?' His mother asks in that manner, the one she uses when he knows she won't like the answer to the question. 'David, do you know anything about the vanishing act of one miniature mediaeval castle with drawbridge, a pirate treasure chest full of gold doubloons, and eight plastic plants?'

He turns and smiles. A parent's joy to behold: the remnants of his dinner – spinach and pea soup – barnacling to his pearl mussel teeth like seaweed, a gap here and there filled with dangling coral gums. No answer. A parent's second nightmare: silence straight from the depths of the ocean floor – wherever that might be.

'Right. No Blue Planet for a week.'

The strangest thing. He smiles again. No argument.

A week later his parents discover a whole cache of missing items: the tv remote control, Tupperware, felt tip pens, shampoo bottles, and pieces of what appear to be moulded drainpipe.

'Our son has turned into a treasure-hunting pirate! Except he's collecting junk,' she laments.

Her husband thinks it is hilarious. Until David's antics spread to school. He comes home one day laden with water bottles, lunchboxes, and a letter from the school's head office. His parents leave the letter on the kitchen table over dinner, cast fleeting glances at it, as if upon opening its paper jaws will rip into the flesh on their hands.

'Da-da-da-da-da-da-da-da,' David's father can't help himself before his wife pokes him gently in the ribcage as she uses a swordfish-like knife to open the envelope.

'Do be serious!'

Dear Mr and Mrs _____,

Your son has taken on the role of Plastics Officer at the school to ensure as little as possible makes its way into the ocean endangering the marine ecosystems therein. Although this endeavour began as a self-appointed role, we can only commend his proactivity and passion. However, we believe it more pertinent to install a special recycling unit on the school premises, despite David's reassurances to his teachers that he has found a 'method of disposal'.

With best wishes,

Ms _____

Head Teacher.

There is a swell of parental pride as they look in on their son before retiring to bed that night. As the dimmer light on the landing ebbs away, a little eel of a boy wriggles with contentment in a bedroom cushioned in waves of plastic, while a few more fish swim in the oceans unhindered.

WARRIOR

F. E. Clark

I WAIT. DARK clad. Ready. I could be arrested for this, locked away—forgotten. They've begun disappearing things, names, people, even history. Life wants to live— sometimes it can, sometimes it cannot.

The day shift has gone now. The sodium lights clunk on, the parking lot is almost empty. I'm a dark ghost. Just a few more minutes, then it will be safe to move.

Checking the box on the passenger seat beside me yet again, I brush my fingers over my beautiful creations. They are perfect—primed and ready. I made them myself. The components are available online, even at grocery stores. The spark and something for it to feed upon—so simple. It wasn't hard to find instructions. In searching I found I was not alone in my goal, all over the planet a network exists. You just need to know how to find it and prove your allegiance.

This is the first location on my list. I've spent a lot of time here, and at places like this, hidden in plain sight.

Pick-ups, drop-offs, mornings, evenings, and weekends—another impatient mother in her beat-up old car, waiting to pick up her child. I've studied the angles, lights, cameras—I know the flow of these places.

Parked in a blind spot, I sit waiting in my cooling car.

THE NIGHT SECURITY guard arrives. Shift changeover. They don't see me as they swagger into the building. It's time. I tuck my hair up beneath my hoodie, exit my car quickly, shielding the box from the cameras. I sprint around the back of the building where heat and fumes of fried food belch into the chill night air.

Moving quickly in the shadows I loop back, entering the parking lot as if I'm a different person. I'm fast, invisible, unstoppable.

I've studied where to hit for maximum impact, aiming for optimum coverage. The first grenade flies arrow-perfect. Noise shatters around the concrete lot. I hit the soft spots, the margins. I carry on throwing until the box is empty. Running for my car, I'm away into the dark before the off-duty security guard leaves.

Come summer, this lot will bloom with cornflowers, buttercups, cowslips, tormentil, forget-me-nots, and poppies. Given the right conditions, seeds will spark and germinate. Life wants to live—I won't let this be forgotten.

I am an eco-warrior.

Author's note: Written in response to reading that The Oxford Junior Dictionary had deleted nature words—particularly the names of flowers.

ACKNOWLEDGEMENTS

STORIES WERE SOURCED via the Green-stories short story competition (www.greenstories.org.uk), run by the University of Southampton, led by Dr Denise Baden, Associate Professor in Sustainable Business from Southampton Business School. Thanks to all of the writers who sent stories, and to our judges Carole Burns (Head of Creative Writing) and Dr. Aiysha Jahan from the University of Southampton.

Grateful thanks also to our final judge Philip Hoare, well-known writer and Professor of Creative Writing at the University of Southampton. Thanks especially to Southampton Business School for funding the prizes. Gratitude is also owed to our volunteer readers Lesley, Melanie, Alistair and Deborah who helped us whittle the entries down.

Look out for future competitions on our website across all formats (film, novel, play, TV etc.) on our website www.greenstories.org.uk and on social media FB: greenstoriessoton, Twitter #GreenstoriesUk and Instagram greenstoriessoton.

Printed in Great Britain
by Amazon

58582598R10142